Andrew St. Mary is a native Californian with deep family roots in Louisiana. As a youth, he was surrounded by a family of storytellers that spurred a love for writing. Now retired, Andrew is able to pursue creating stories that inspire and excite young readers and those young at heart. His first co-authored book in what will be a series is '*The Sitka Adventure-Journey to New Helvetia*'.

I dedicate this book to my beautiful wife, Sonya, for her steadfast support of my writing pursuits and who inspires me in everything I do.

I also dedicate this work to my loving family, including three extraordinary children: my sons Esteban and Christopher and daughter Taylor, my grandchildren Ayla and Glovanni (the inspiration for Gio Jr.)

They inspire and challenge me to live life to the fullest.

Andrew St Mary

THE SITKA ADVENTURE –
RETURN TO YERBA BUENA

AUSTIN MACAULEY PUBLISHERS™

LONDON • CAMBRIDGE • NEW YORK • SHARJAH

Ordering Information
Quantity sales: Special discounts are available on quantity purchases by corporations, associations, and others. For details, contact the publisher at the address below.

Publisher's Cataloging-in-Publication data
St Mary, Andrew
The Sitka Adventure – Return To Yerba Buena

ISBN 9798891552227 (Paperback)
ISBN 9798891552340 (ePub e-book)

Library of Congress Control Number: 2023924206

www.austinmacauley.com/us

First Published 2024
Austin Macauley Publishers LLC
40 Wall Street, 33rd Floor, Suite 3302
New York, NY 10005
USA

mail-usa@austinmacauley.com
+1 (646) 5125767

Thanks to my big brother Levy for his multiple reviews and feedback on this writing journey. Also, thanks to him and my sister-in-law, Judy, for serving as my test audience for readings. I offer heartfelt thanks to longtime friends Mark Ginsberg and Gary Levinson-Palmer for their unbiased, thoughtful suggestions and unwavering support. Thanks once more to Nathaniel Wiley, student extraordinaire, for his review of this second book in the Sitka series. I want to again recognize my very special friend and mentor, Dr. Kevin O Starr (1940–2017), Ph.D. in American literature from Harvard University, unparalleled historian, author and California State Librarian Emeritius (2004) (aka Owen Owen Owl), and his wife Sheila Starr, who continue to support my writing endeavors.

Table of Contents

Chapter 1
Fate or Premonition

Early next morning, Father gently shook my arm, whispering, "SHHH, wake up, Elsu, wake up, time to go." I saw he was wearing his hunting clothes, so I got excited. "Get your gear and meet me outside," he said. "Today we hunt, but I don't want to wake Grandfather. He needs his rest today, and we need to hunt." So, quickly and quietly, I got dressed, grabbed my bow, and tiptoed past Grandpa to meet Father outside.

I must admit, I did feel a little guilty about ditching Grandpa, but I really wanted to go hunting with Father. So, as we sneaked down to our canoe, we were surprised to find him already sitting in it.

Father spoke first, "Grandfather, should you not rest today? We return late this evening after traveling over many hills, through forest, and upriver for game. It will be tiring, and I worry for your well-being. Please join us this evening that Elsu may hear more of your incredible experiences."

But Grandpa would have none of that, saying, "I will join you today, Enyeto! I hunted and trapped this region long before you could crawl. I know the spirits that live with the land. Every hill, tree, river, and scent is part of my being.

To have my grandson join you on this hunt without me is misguided. You will not deny me this experience with him." I could tell from his tone he was annoyed, and as we knew, Grandfather Liwanu was not one to be dismissed.

My father looked carefully into Grandpa's eyes and quickly conceded to his elder, saying, "Yes, Father, forgive my foolishness. We are honored that you join us and can teach Elsu a thing or two about the land upon which we hunt and fish. I will fetch your gear and more supplies." Grandpa dismissed Father with a wave of his hand, then shifted closer to me in the canoe to chat. "Your father sees me as just a feeble old warrior now, but never forget, age is not a good measure of one's spirit, strength, or usefulness." Then, with his hand on my right shoulder and a twinkle in his eye, he whispered, "I am not yet spent, Elsu." I considered his words and wondered if that principle applied to young people like me. As Grandpa spoke, I could smell the faint aroma of lavender he stashed in his waist pouch. I did not understand his connection to lavender, but its fragrance always made me think he was nearby.

When Father returned, Mother was with him. I figured the discussion about Grandpa tagging along on the hunting trip was not yet finished. I was wrong. Mama just hugged Grandpa and asked him to keep me safe. At ten years old, I did not realize the significance of that moment, but later I would.

We loaded extra gear in the canoe and shoved off with Grandpa nestled in the back, his eyes closed, napping as Father, and I began to row upriver. Though I knew after an exhausting day of hunting, the smooth downstream return trip would not further tax our already sore bodies, I also knew that the price for that luxury was to fight the steady current as we paddled upstream. Though our progress was slow, and my forehead glistened with sweat, the journey was made easier by the delightful sounds of songbirds muffling the sound of our canoe cutting through the water. An occasional grunt from animals on shore prompted me to grab my bow. But Father counseled me, saying, "Patience Elsu, patience. We shall see them soon enough." So upriver we continued, Grandpa Liwanu, Father, and me. Life couldn't be sweeter, and I could feel myself smiling for this moment in time.

About an hour passed, and I was getting restless. "We almost there?" I asked Father for at least the hundredth time.

"Soon, Elsu, Soon," he responded, dismissing me with a wave of his hand. *Like father, like son,* I thought.

A short while later, he pointed to a landing spot ahead. *Here we go*, I thought as I grabbed my gear. I glanced at Grandpa, and he was doing the same. "I'll help you with your gear if you want, Grandpa," I asked. Another dismissive wave came my way. *Guess I'd better get used to that.*

As we climbed out of our canoe, Father reminded me how difficult returning home would be if it went missing during the hunt. I pointed to some dense bushes that looked like a good place to stash the canoe. After dragging it behind the cover and looking around the area to get our bearings, I helped Father unload the nets and baskets. Then the three of us carried everything else to a spot at the edge of the woods where we set up base camp for the day. The sun was rising in the east, and patchy clouds filtered the heat, creating a perfect day for fishing, so Grandpa and I headed to the river.

I was determined to impress Grandpa Liwanu. "C'mon, Grandpa, watch me catch a big one," I yelled. "C'mon, the big ones are getting away." But he had already found a comfortable tree stump to rest from all the rowing he didn't do on the way.

While Father was busy organizing camp, I wasted no time wading ankle-deep in the river looking to spear my trophy fish. The river's current was not too strong near the shore, and the cool water felt good on my legs. Beyond the river, I saw dense forest and could hear branches on the trees creaking and the melody of leaves kissing as they rustled in the gentle breeze. The reflections of wispy clouds floating against a blue sky danced on the river's rippled surface. My commune with nature was broken when Father shouted, "Not too far, hunter boy. Don't leave our view." I sort of heard Father and sort of not. "ELSU!" he shouted. I definitely heard that and responded with a wave of my hand. *Oh no, did I just do that?*

With that last exchange, Father disappeared into the woods to set some traps leaving Grandpa Liwanu in my custody or vice versa. I wasn't sure and didn't care while eying the biggest salmon I'd ever seen cruising upriver. *Say hello to hunter boy*, I murmured, moving in for the kill. Focusing my eyes on the water's surface, I spied the fish heading upstream. As I tracked him like a shadow, I was amazed by his size and the rainbow colors that reflected from his wet, shiny body. With spear in hand silently, I began my approach, ready to thrust.

Suddenly, I noticed a much larger shadow, a grisly shadow just ahead. Armed with just a boy-sized spear, I froze in fear gazing up at the massive bear standing before me. A warm stream snaked from my crotch down my leg to the river. The bear's head was the size of a giant pumpkin that grew in our village garden. Its claws were longer and sharper than the finest arrowheads made by our tribe's warriors. Its black fur was darker than the coals in the tribe's fire pit the morning after a ceremonial fire dance.

One thing I'd learned from hunting with Grandpa, Father, and warriors from our village is to stay connected to nature and my surroundings. Just as there is game, there are threats. The trick is not to become game. Any warrior hunter worth his salt knew and lived by this.

To be caught off-guard meant one was not breathing in nature and all its complexity; the fragrance of wildflowers scenting the air, the smell of the earth, the aroma of animal scents on the wind whistling around tree trunks and rustling the leaves, all nature's sounds blending like an orchestra. And my duty was to avoid threats in this ever-changing environment. Failure to heed this lesson was taboo for any Miwok, even young ones.

I was ashamed that, in my excitement, I had ignored my surroundings. And, I'd strayed too far from Grandpa Liwanu's view and protection. Part of me felt I deserved what was soon coming. As the bear studied me, I feared it was trying to figure out which meal was bigger or tastier, the salmon it had just caught or me. She wouldn't need a fish with a full-size ten-year-old boy to feast on. So, even with a large fish tucked in her mouth, her growl told me I would be an ample substitute for dinner. Then oddly, she turned as if distracted by an important, powerful spirit. I hoped she'd spotted another dinner substitute, but that's not what caught her attention. I was terrified to move, shivering in a pickle of my own making.

It's funny what you think of when the end is near. Right then, all I could think of was how much I loved my mom and all she'd done for me. I wished I could see her and say, *"I love you, Mom, and I'm so sorry."*

It seemed like an eternity, but finally, when I got the nerve to look around, I shifted from fear to total shock. Standing there deadlocked in a stare-down with this behemoth was Grandpa Liwanu, standing perfectly still but looking larger than I ever saw him before. *We're both goners now,* I figured, but once again, I was wrong. Then, I thought, *Maybe he's distracting her, trying to save me. So, I should run. But I couldn't leave Grandpa, especially when this was my fault. But I'll never see Mother again if I don't run.* Quite a crossroad for a ten-year-old, but deep down inside, a voice told me what to do.

Slowly, I shifted to Grandpa's side to go down with him. Though I could see the bear tracking my movement with her fist-sized eyes, she did not move toward us. "Bow Elsu," Grandpa whispered. I guess I didn't react quickly enough, so he repeated, "Bow," with his right hand now pressing down on my left shoulder. Together we bowed before the bear, then Grandpa stood tall, pulling me up beside him. Even at ten years old, this seemed like a big mistake. But then, the mother bear bowed and placed the fish at Grandpa's feet.

For a moment that seemed to last forever, the bear looked him squarely and respectfully in the eyes. The two of them acted as if they were sharing a common dream. Then, as suddenly as the bear appeared, she turned away toward the forest and jumped ashore with so much force that a wave of water smacked me sideways, almost causing me to fall.

Once she was out of sight, my knees buckled, and I gasped for air as I dropped to the ground, speechless, not believing what just happened. Grandpa leaned over, picked up the fish, then looked at me and joked, "Elsu, what did you catch?" *Seems like I just scratched the surface about Miwok's bond with Mother Earth.* Then, in a more serious tone, he said, "What a fine gift the bear offers us. Thank her when we cook the fish on the fire. Perhaps later, the village will honor her with the Uzumati dance."

"The Uzi what?" I asked.

"The Uzumati," he repeated, explaining that it was a grizzly bear ceremony and I could dress up like a bear cub. "Till then, Elsu, it's our secret."

I think Grandpa was trying to calm me as my knees were still shaking, and my stomach was in a knot. Finally, when I did calm down, I asked, "Grandpa, what just happened? Why did that bear give you her catch and leave like that? We were goners."

"Let us fish, hunter boy," was all he would say. Since I knew it was not wise to push Grandpa for an explanation, I decided to join him at the river. Though I had not gotten that monster salmon out of my head yet, I had to admit that encounter with the bear really shook me, an experience I would not forget for the rest of my life.

Several minutes passed before I got the nerve to resume my fish hunt, making sure of my surroundings this time. Again, spear in hand, I maneuvered through the water seeking the big one while Grandpa sat on a boulder near the shore smiling, or maybe smirking. Thanks to him, I did feel more fearless. The fish must have heard the loud thumping of my heart after that encounter with the bear, swimming away from the point of my spear. I failed to catch any fish at all. "I tried, Grandpa, but I am not the hunter boy you thought I was."

I figured we'd go back to meet Father at camp, but Grandpa rose from his seat, took some weird-looking bulbs from his waist pouch, and handed them to me. "Go now, Elsu, place these waste deep in the water and wait. You will then know the wisdom of our forefathers."

"Ok, Grandpa, if you say so." I placed the bulbs in the water as told and waited for what I didn't know.

A few minutes later, the giant salmon I spotted earlier and several other fish darted to the bulbs to nibble. And like magic, suddenly, they lay still in the water, unable to move. "Now, Elsu! Now!" yelled Grandpa. Once, twice, three times, I thrust my spear, retrieving a big one each time. "Now we have dinner, Elsu. Let us go; your father will worry." I loaded the fish in the basket Mother had woven just for that purpose, but it was a little too heavy for me to carry alone. So, Grandpa grabbed one of the side handles and me the other.

As we walked, I couldn't help noticing how slow and feeble he seemed when he looked eight feet tall in front of that bear a little earlier. Grandpa was a brave, fearless warrior, and I admired him. He always told me, "Elsu, don't try to be like the others you see. Just try to be whom you are meant to be. All you will ever need; you will find inside you."

I swore to myself that such wisdom would not be wasted. I tried to lift my side of the basket a little higher to ease the weight on his side. We passed some bramble bushes loaded with raspberries, so I stopped and picked some to eat with our fish. But really, I wanted to give Grandpa a break from lugging the heavy basket. Right then and there, I promised myself to look out for him the same way he looked out for me.

When we returned to camp, Father was already preparing some wild game hens and a rabbit he'd caught in the woods for roasting. "Well, what have we here," he exclaimed. He was clearly impressed by our catch. We sat around the embers from the roasting fire for a spell with full tummies. Then we packed the rest for home. I was glad Grandpa Liwanu joined us. I realized I had lots to learn from him. And I was curious about those bulbs but much more about that bear.

Father and I loaded the gear and leftover food on the canoe while Grandpa relaxed by the smoldering embers. Once we finished, I darted over to ask him again about the goings-on with that bear by the river. But the embers' dwindling heat with the faint lavender aroma from his waist pouch had nearly put him to sleep. "Grandpa, Grandpa," I called softly, trying not to startle him.

"Hey, hunter boy, time to go?"

"Almost, Grandpa, but what about that bear and the fish?" I whispered.

"Yes, Elsu, she knew it was my time, not hers. I promise you will understand one day, but now you must show patience. All becomes clear in time." I did not understand the meaning of Grandpa Liwanu's words, but I trusted what he said. That I would in time.

As dusk approached, we boarded our canoe and left for home. It was a smoother trip downriver, and we all sat in the canoe like conquerors with the game and great fish we caught. *Mama will be pleased*, I thought. When we got home, she was especially delighted with the already roasted portions ready for dinner. I was still pretty excited about fishing and that encounter with the bear. Neither Grandpa nor I mentioned that part to my parents. I asked him if he would continue his story about Will and the Sitka crew, but Mother cut me off, saying, "I'm sure Grandfather can use a good night's sleep. Perhaps he'll share more in the morning." Grandpa nodded, meaning yes, so I dropped my request for now but was still restless.

"Play with me, Father," I begged, still needing to burn off some energy.

"Sure, hunter boy, how about shinny, one on one."

"Yea, that's my favorite." So, Father and I headed for the village grounds while Grandpa retired to the hut sensing all was as it should be. Soon he would dream of his youth and his precious Papina.

Chapter 2
Unexpected Outcome

As the morning dawned bright and sunny, I shot out of bed and made a beeline for our story tree. Grandpa was already seated on the pine needles, slurping some kind of hot liquid from his favorite cup with steam rising from the top. But first, Mother motioned for me to come eat. "Where's Father?" I asked.

"He's down by the river cleaning out the canoe. He said he'd return by the time Grandpa got started. You know he doesn't want to miss one word of what Grandfather Liwanu has to say this morning."

Anxiously, I sat snacking on sweet, juicy blueberries and some leftover roasted rabbit from last night's dinner. Every few minutes, I peered down the path to the river from which Father would be coming. While waiting, I again thought about the incident with that bear. I felt proud of the decision I made to stand with Grandpa Liwanu. To not run away in the face of the greatest threat I'd ever known though I was terrified and sure we'd met our end. Also, I felt fortunate and thankful for surviving my encounter with the bear and bringing home the fish she offered to Grandpa and me. You never know how things may turn out, so I figured one day at a time. Finally, seeing Father walking back, I wolfed down the rest of my breakfast and rushed to the tree to get my spot on the pine needles beside Grandpa. I even tucked some berries and dried deer meat in my waste pouch to snack on later.

Once Papa got comfortable, Grandpa picked up talking right where he had left off. "Now, remember yesterday I said Will had his crew get a good night's sleep, and he drifted off to sleep dreaming of exotic places? Well, the next morning was not anything like Will imagined it would be. An aroma of uncertainty spread across the Sitka that next morning and calamity was in the air. The brightening sunrise stripped the crew of night's dark cover, meaning they could no longer avoid being seen. The figures of their bodies joined the early morning shadows of trees on the calm waters. They were dangerously exposed in plain view of the humans out in mass on a day like this. A dilemma even the most incredible pondering could not cure. All the crew felt it. Jonathan Fox stood erect, tilted his head sniffing, trying to make sense of it all. At the same time, Gio and family cringed inside the stuffy little cabin."

Grandpa Liwanu paused for a minute and turned to me, saying, "You know, Elsu, I learned from my father Hanta how to blend in with the woods, hills, and streams when I was a boy to hunt and trap. He also taught me about the bulbs to fish with. In the water, they stun the fish for a little bit so you can grab them. He taught me many things, but I don't recall him ever having to deal with boatloads of those ignorant and hostile to our way of life. I felt sorry for Will the bear, as traveling unnoticed was no longer an option for them. But being a daring captain, it was no surprise to me he took matters into his own paws."

Turning back to the three of us, he continued.

Then, with great courage and audacity, Will commanded, "Akoni, we need as much speed as we can muster. Fire up that boiler. Rev up the engine. The rest of you, take the oars. Full steam ahead." Standing tall and stout, he pointed upriver toward the New Helvetia Riverfront. With his head tilted forward, shoulders arched in defiance, and fur shimmering in the sunlight, Will looked like a giant inspiring the crew to rediscover their courage. It felt like they were charging into battle; again.

I know, secretly, Will hoped they would slide past the main dock unnoticed. But I'm sure he was prepared for the worst.

They hadn't ventured far before being confronted by a bunch of gun-toting humans in their boats. Vastly outnumbered and not knowing what to expect, Will brought the Sitka to a full halt. Then he headed for the bow to confront the furless hoard.

None of the crew had ever been in such close contact with humans. They were confused by all the odd scents and more than a little terrified by the armed faction. Thankfully, no guns were pointed at any of them for the moment. The poor rabbit family, now hiding behind the stout legs of Captain Will, peeked at the humans hoping they wouldn't be on the menu for that evening's dinner.

Gio Jr. had never smelled any humans before and wasn't sure what to make of it. Unfortunately, though, he could tell from his parents' nervous trembling that things were not good.

"I'm scared, Mama," he whispered.

Jenny reassured him, "Don't worry, my son. Mama loves you and won't let anything happen to you," soothing words for a shaky situation.

Jonathan Fox had already planned to jump off near the stern of the Sitka and bolt to the nearby woods if things got dicey. For the moment, though, he stood his ground to avoid causing anyone to panic, whispering to the rest of the crew, "Careful, careful." Amos positioned himself next to Will, ready for action knowing his tail was an ample response for anything the humans might throw at them. From their vantage point in the sky, the flyers could view any threatening movements in the boats and signal the crew to abandon ship and escape. Sasha was monitoring the situation from the water on the starboard side of the Sitka.

With his keen bear senses, Captain Will reasoned that a friendly gesture might ease the tension. So, much to the crew's surprise, he yelled "Ahoy, mates."

"Ahoy, mates!" Jonathan repeated to Jenny in a mocking tone. "He does realize those are humans over there. Humans!" He grumbled in a voice dripping with sarcasm.

Jenny shushed Jonathan and scolded him, saying, "Have faith in our captain."

The rest of the crew froze and held their breath. Joaquin Hawk and Owen Owl were circling, ready to attack from above if necessary. They had come through too much together to desert now, even in the face of overwhelming odds. The question was, how would the humans react? An uncomfortable silence set in as Will waited for their response.

The humans stood tall in their boats, looking curiously at and taking stock of the impressive animal crew before them. It was a standoff. "Like with that bear, Grandpa?" I let slip out. "What bear?" asked Mama, with Father looking puzzled at Grandpa, who just brushed them off and kept talking. On the third boat back, some of John's hands were captivated, staring at a steamboat manned by an odd collection of animals that usually co-exist as prey or predator in the wild. "Lookee there, they even have a beaver," Marco quipped to the others in his boat, pointing at Sasha in the water, eyeing them.

What was Jonathan Fox thinking? "Last time something like this happened, things got out of hand fast." Gio Jr. positioned himself by his dad's side, ready for action this time. Then, in the lead boat, a few humans seem to be whispering to each other. Finally, one of them stepped forward to address Will directly. Amos Skunk was thinking, *Perhaps he's their captain. Well, they better watch their step unless they want a dose of my special gift, and I've got more gifts than a Christmas tree.* "Ha, ha," laughed Grandpa with smiling eyes.

"Did Amos Skunk really say that?" asked Father.

"Okay," said Grandpa. "I just threw that part in about the Christmas gifts."

But then, Father added, "Well, years ago, I encountered one of Amos the skunk's family, and I can tell you it was no Christmas gift I received."

Mother added, "It certainly was not," We all howled with laughter till Grandpa silenced us to continue the story.

Now, Captain John, who stepped forward, was, in fact, their leader. So, he spoke to Will first. "Ahoy there, I'm

John, leader of this colony. We own most of the grazing and farmland in this region. I couldn't help but notice that one of your crew there," looking directly at Gio Rabbit, "has an off-colored brown foot."

Captain Will was stunned. That was not what he expected from their captain. And no one had ever mentioned that before about Gio. Captain John continued, "Yesterday, my guard dogs Lance and Terrance reported a big skirmish with those awful coyotes. Those varmints have been terrorizing our livestock and fields for years. Lance also reported being helped by a group of newcomers to these parts. One of them was a ferocious rabbit with an off-colored brown foot just like him," again pointing at Gio. "Is that him?" Will answered that it was.

"Well then, welcome," exclaimed John, both arms raised high. "You're among friends here."

I tell you, Will wasn't sure what to think since humans were famous for trading animal pelts, not pleasantries with the likes of them. And at 8 feet tall with thick brown fur, he did not want to become someone's rug or overcoat. He had already gravely misjudged Calvin and didn't want to repeat the same mistake, especially with humans.

"Give me just a moment," Will responded, then turned to consult the crew. Akoni spoke first, reminding them that humans had lied to them and could not be trusted. Jonathan and Sasha were frightened and could not form words to express their feelings.

Then the voice of reasoning, Jenny Rabbit, chimed in. "My grandfather always advised me that while it's best to keep your friends close, one should keep your enemies even closer to you." That expression settled Captain Will's thinking on the matter. He waved Captain John on board the Sitka. As a gesture of good faith, John accepted and joined Captain Will as the other humans nervously looked on. Will reached out a paw, and John reached out a hand. A unique partnership forged between two groups that couldn't be more different.

"That's quite a boat you've got there," said John. "Never seen a steam-powered vessel in these parts before. Heard a lot about them from Harper over there. He's from Liverpool, England, and has lots of tales about steamboats. Say, why don't you and your shipmates join us for dinner this evening at our main settlement just over yonder (pointing at some buildings)? We'd be honored if you did. And, perhaps you'll do me the courtesy of allowing me to ride back to camp aboard your splendid vessel?" With most of his crew signaling their encouragement, Captain Will consented. So, off they went to a fascinating evening.

There they were, unexpected hosts, unusual guests, in unfamiliar surroundings. The large, heavily fortified adobe building with a great hearth stove in the corner, drenching the room with warmth and comfort, seemed most inviting to Will and the crew. And spread out before them was a feast fit for a king.

"Or a bear?" I added, drawing a little grin from Grandpa as he went on.

I'm sure Jonathan Fox was probably thinking, *I hope they're not trying to fatten us up.* Jenny was confused by all the plants indoors that should be growing outdoors.

Captain John walked over and sat beside Will, stationed near the stove warming his backside. Sasha Beaver was busy studying its construction. "I just wanted to thank you and your group again for their bravery at the crop fields." Then, with a twinge of emotion, he confessed, "my dogs could not have handled that many coyotes on their own. I'm forever in your debt. Lance and Terrance are very special to me. I raised them from pups and couldn't bear losing either of them. So, what can I do to repay you?" And with that question, Captain Will began to ponder very carefully.

After a short while, he replied, "Thank you and your villagers for your warm and generous hospitality." Then, he stated very firmly, "For starters, I guess we'd like not to join those stuffed heads hanging over that big mantle over there or become part of one of your boat shipments. I'm sure I speak for the entire crew on that matter."

"Of course," replied John. "You're my special guests. None of my people would dare think of harming you or your crew."

Then, John became more insistent, asking, "But Captain Will, what do you want? What do you need?"

Will thought a bit more, scratching his head before replying, "Sasha and Owen sometimes have trouble seeing and could use some spectacles. Also, it gets really cold in the winter, so Gio and his family need blankets to keep warm."

John agreed but kept prodding Will, saying, "No problem, Captain, but what about you? What do you need? There must be something?"

With no tree trunk available to scratch, Will had to think quickly on his feet. "Alright," he finally said. "I need a settlement area here to start a trade business."

Grandpa paused to ask us, "Now, why would a group of animals want to start a trade business?" After several minutes of scattered mumbling, it was evident that none of us had the slightest clue. So, we all sat there blank-faced, staring at Grandpa, who had a smug look, gratified that no one could answer his little riddle.

We waited for him to answer, but he would not be rushed. Instead, he moved with the speed of a weary tortoise. So, there he sat nibbling on a dough ball and sipping a hot beverage Mama made from pepperwood berries. I even tried to get him to give me a sip trying to speed him up. But I quickly realized I was swimming upstream as Grandpa would not be rushed for an answer. Instead, he purposefully took even more time to stretch out his arms and legs after finishing his treats.

Finally, after what seemed like an hour, Grandpa told us how Will mysteriously arrived at Yerba Buena Island from across the seas with nothing but an old worn sailor's bag. In it were some clothes and other personal items, among them several coins and a few small trinkets, none of which made any sense to Will. Grandpa described how Will felt these things might be important, so he slept with the bag to protect them while dreaming he was some kind of shrewd wheeler dealer. This recurring dream consumed him as much as our village warriors embrace their sacred vow to defend our village against threats. His restless and adventurous nature fed his yearning to know who he was. Finally, it drove him to convince his closest friends to join him on a journey to unknown destinations seeking fame and fortune and, hopefully, some answers about his past.

I can tell you it didn't take long for Will and Jenny Rabbit to figure out that a trade business would be a boon to ensuring safety for them and animals at large.

"A lot was riding on this trade deal," warned Grandpa. "Humans can't even get along with humans, let alone animals, even talking ones. And talking animals operating a trade business? That might be a mountain too high."

Anyway, Will told John they hoped to start that small trade business and could use his help to keep other humans from interfering. "To make this work, we'll need your permission to harvest crops from your fields occasionally," he told John. "But I'm sure you noticed our boat is small, as is our crew, so we can't harvest too much. Just enough to share with family and friends back home on Yerba Buena Island and maybe finance some additional trips."

"Of course, we're willing to share any profits, and we can help around the settlement when we're here. Perhaps we could assist Lance and Terrance with guard duty. They are wonderful animals, and we have the utmost respect for them. But our flyers can scout from the sky and have keen eyesight at night. And Amos, well, let's say he has a gift for repelling intruders."

Grandpa took a moment to throw a sly grin Father's way. Then, we all chuckled again at Father's mishap way back with a skunk.

"I must say my relationship with most animals has been as a hunter and trapper," said Father. "But if I came across animals that could speak, I would have to reconsider everything I know about hunting or learned from you, Father," who nodded without comment. I knew I would think a lot about what Father had just said. I would think a lot about Gio Jr. and all the Sitka crew. They had become close to me like family through Grandpa's saga. Grandpa made one of those throat-clearing sounds to silence us as he continued.

Captain John asked Will, "How about I just set you up in a place right near mine? That way, you can coordinate with Lance and Terrance. I would be honored to have good neighbors like you and your crew. I'll have my men tidy the place up and patch the roof to keep you all dry during storms. Please make arrangements with Lance and Terrance to help with local security. The pastures are nearby, where you can harvest what you need for your trade business. And I guarantee no one will bother you or they will answer to me," flashing his sidearm. "There's even an opening in the attic where your flyers should be comfortable and can go and come as they please."

"That's mighty gracious of you," replied Will. "Sounds like the beginnings of a profitable partnership. I'll inform my crew."

At this point, the crew was busy feasting on every type of fruit, steamed vegetables, and smoked meats imaginable. The humans were busy enjoying their own specially formulated concoction that seemed to add some extra pizzazz to the festivities. Amos Skunk even brought out the jug of elixir he found on the wreckage.

"What does axlir mean?" I asked.

"It's called e-lix-ir," enunciated Grandpa. When they all glanced at each other, I could tell it was not a drink for my age.

"It was a night of nights for them. In truth, no one was more relieved than the crew about not shoving off aboard the Sitka in the morning. Especially after six-plus days on the river dealing with all kinds of dangerous mishaps," said Grandpa.

As Owen Owl offered a toast, Jonathan Fox muttered, "Not another long speech."

"Now, family, I tell you that Owen was quite the speaker. I will try to say it the way Owen said it, but I may not say it the same as Owen."

"Hello and bonjour, our esteemed New Helvetian hosts. We convey our gratitude for your impeccable hospitality worthy of royalty, least of all your wayward guests. May our joyful consumption of this special meal show our gratitude not only for the lavish feast set before us but equally for the kindness extended by your villagers. Thus, we are compelled to extend an invitation to grace our precious Yerba Buena Island that we may return the favor with a culinary masterpiece of our own. The most comfortable accommodations will be provided, set against the panoramic communion of the distant city and expansive ocean, wherein the aquatic and terrestrial worlds collide. Your arrival will be cause for jubilant celebration." Owen then offered, "Cheers," as everyone raised their cups.

"Wow! I don't know what he said, but that was a superb toast, a real dandy," commented Harper in his unmistakable English accent. "Cheers to Owen and hail the Queen," he stammered in a state induced by the liquid libations reserved for the humans.

It was the kind of evening that spawns enduring bonds and friendships, something desperately needed by Will's group, who longed for the closeness of family and friends and the familiarity of home.

I could see Mother a little teary-eyed when Grandpa said that. So, I moved over and put my hand in hers, asking, "You ok, Mama?"

She smiled at me and said, "Yes, Elsu, Mama is fine. Those words about family touched me. They made me think of my parents and our family. These are happy tears, my son, not sad ones." As I glanced at Father, I thought I saw a little trickle down his face too. Even Grandpa seemed moved, shielding his face from our view. Grandpa was a proud warrior, and I loved him.

He went on to explain that Captain Will and the crew retired to their new quarters once the merrymaking fizzled. It was quite a unique experience being indoors without needing a Sasha Beaver campfire, given the large stone fireplace already ablaze, casting heat throughout.

"I could get too used to this," commented Jonathan Fox, stretched out, curling his toes on a comfy rug near the blaze.

But Will cautioned them all, saying, "Remember, this is our camp, not our home. For sometimes, we lose sight of where home truly is." Everyone nodded in agreement, especially Jenny Rabbit, who never was sold on this trip in the first place. We nodded in agreement too.

With no need for watch duty in their new digs, the whole crew settled in for a restful night's sleep, not knowing that the immediate future would be anything but restful.

Chapter 3
Quest for Gold

The morning blossomed a brilliant sun over a speckled sky like an alarm clock signaling to the crew; time to rise. However, still dazed and recovering from the previous night's festivities, they moved to less-lit nooks and crannies to continue their slumber. With a big, bearish yawn, Will asked Sasha to toss more logs on the fire. Then, after a few shifts and groans, they all curled up for some extra shuteye.

"Being a bunch of forest critters," Grandpa said, trying to stifle a laugh, "their snoring was like an unruly symphony with everyone chiming in."

Lance and Terrance could hear it over by the pastures where they'd just arrived to start their daily chores. "Better not wake them just yet," said Lance.

"Yeah, they had a long evening," snickered Terrance. "I doubt we're gonna see coyotes or any other varmints anytime soon after that big skirmish. Anyway, the field hands are still busy cleaning up the clutter and replanting."

"Hey, let's go visit Miner Mike," suggested Lance. "He's always good for a laugh." Miner Mike was an old hermit living in a one-room shack eking out a living panning for gold in the river beds winding through the foothills.

"Grandpa, did you ever pan for gold?" I asked.

Grandfather Liwanu became very serious in addressing that question. "Elsu, our people accepted what Mother Earth offered. Her gifts, like gold, were plentiful, but we used them only for our livelihood, not to enrich our existence. For generations, our people honored Mother Earth. And in return, she has taken us to her bosom, nurturing us as a mother would a child. She shares gifts far beyond gold, like the precious lavender flower, its clean, sweet scent easing our woes and soothing our ills. So many of her plants and herbs not only sustain but heal us."

"The wild lavender I keep over my bed and in my pouch keeps me sturdy and keen. Its floral aroma soothes me to sleep. Mother Earth has always been our benefactress; we are bound to be hers. This duty is not only tradition but the duty of all humanity to be stewards of Mother Earth. Do you understand, Elsu?"

"I think so, Grandpa. We must love and care for Mother Earth as family." Grandpa just smiled and patted me on the top of my head. I think he was pleased with my answer.

It was now late morning as Grandfather Liwanu described the remarkable calm that enveloped the valley that day. Butterflies fluttered about, and ladybugs dotted the landscape. Bees buzzed flowers for pollen while squirrels scampered about playfully. Birds of every type, size, and color filled the air with chirps, tweets, and humming, with even an occasional rat-a-tat-tat from some woodpeckers joining in the chorus almost on beat. Even some crickets, beetles, and other insects chimed in with their own unique clicking sounds.

Lance and Terrance were en route to Miner Mike's while the Sitka crew was barely stirring to life. No sooner than Captain Will heaved open the heavy wooden front door, sunlight invaded every corner and crevice of their cabin, leaving nowhere to hide. "Guess we better get up," moaned Jonathan Fox. Anticipating they might need a lift; Captain John had a table full of goodies delivered for breakfast. After some serious munching, they stretched a bit more and finally moseyed outside. Even the flyers avoided flying for now. All said and done; it was an easygoing, lazy day.

By this time, Lance and Terrance had comfortably positioned themselves within range to snicker at Miner Mike's humorous gold-panning antics. No one quite knew where Mike came from or even how old he was, except according to Lance, he was as hairy as Terrance but not as well-groomed and with a worse scent. Still, every sunrise with his sidekick mule Ovie, he could be found at the river's edge setting up equipment for the long, arduous task of gold-panning. As usual, Ovie stood near the shore, neck lowered, munching on tall wild grass shoots and any other vegetation available.

Gold-panning was Miner Mike's life. He dreamed of someday finding that one magical nugget that would be his claim to fame. In the meantime, to get by, he and Ovie survived on the generosity of Captain John routinely ignoring their occasional visits to the pastures and smokehouse. But, if Mike did strike gold, it was on John's land anyway.

While Lance and Terrance entertained themselves at Miner Mike's expense, the Sitka crew lounged about outside their cabin most of the day, snacking and relaxing. A false sense of security was beginning to take hold that only Will and Jenny seemed to grasp. The flyers spent most of their time in the air, so they kept a better connection to the region beyond the compound. But the other crew members clearly and unwisely had lessened their guard.

At the New Helvetia settlement, the humans weren't too energetic themselves and even slower to rise.

"Because of that elixir juice?" I asked. Grandpa just smiled, which made me smile.

Before the Sitka crew realized it, a week had come and gone. With all the tasty food unloaded from their boat plus what Captain John provided, they dined in fashion every evening in the warmth and comfort of their home away from home. As promised by Captain John, other humans kept their distance. But they had all gotten a little too comfortable. And they had begun snapping at each other, a clear sign of boredom. Jonathan was too bossy, and Owen kept correcting everyone.

Captain Will worried they were falling into the same humdrum routine as on Yerba Buena Island. *I've got to call a meeting; snap us out of this, but it can wait till morning,* Will murmured to himself, yawning into a deep slumber.

The next morning found the sun vacated by dark, edgy clouds resembling creatures from a horror tale. With the backdrop of rugged, snow-tipped mountains, an eerie sense of unearthliness was in the air. I snuggled closer to Mama as Grandpa continued, using his voice for scary effect. Patchy damp fog and musty, algae-covered soil only added to the mystique. Finally, the crew, relaxing inside their warm quarters, reluctantly followed Captain Will's orders and headed toward the apple grove for the meeting, grumbling all the way. Will had arrived earlier to locate a trunk to scratch and think before the meeting.

Once the crew arrived, Captain Will spoke, gesturing with his right paw. "My friends, first, let me express my gratitude and appreciation for your loyalty, courage, and contribution to the success of this important expedition. We have already come through so much together. Your continued commitment to discovery and exploration for the benefit of our fellow Yerba Buenians is humbling. I've called this meeting to present you with an incredible proposition. A new venture likely to secure a prosperous future for us and family though not without risk and uncertainty." The crew was now fully attentive, hanging on Will's every word, and he could sense that as he strolled among them in confident strides gesturing with both paws to cement his points.

"I am speaking to you about (then Will paused to arouse their curiosity even more before saying) GOLD!" Sensing puzzlement among the crew, he repeated, "Yes, gold. I've been hearing the humans whispering among themselves all week about it. Seems it has untold value. But they can't find it. So, they're relying on some old miner to find it for them. That's where we come in."

Akoni Raccoon still didn't get it saying, "If they can't find it, how will we?"

"Well," explained Will, "the outdoors is our natural habitat. We can get to places the humans can't. We even have flyers, and Sasha Beaver can search underwater. So tomorrow, bright and early, I propose we head to the foothills with the maps from the shipwreck. The humans won't miss a few picks and shovels from the tool shed."

Following some healthy back and forth, the re-energized crew exclaimed, "We're with you, Captain." Their new venture, dubbed 'Sitka's Quest for Gold', was officially underway. They agreed to sneak off before sunrise the following day to the foothills, armed with picks and shovels, to seek their fortune.

Grandpa added, "I am sure the nocturnal crew members had no problem leaving before sunrise. However, I am unsure about the rest of the crew since, after dinner, they relaxed around the fireplace, gloating about striking gold and what they would do with it. They should have been getting a good night's sleep as I would have."

"There is a lesson here, Elsu. One must be well rested and alert when pursuing a quest into the unknown. But, as I said, instead of resting, the lure of gold had infected their thinking."

Sasha Beaver figured he could have his own personal tea kettle sculpted entirely of gold. Gio Rabbit imagined a golden bust of himself in a running position to commemorate his victory over the guard dogs prompting a scornful glance from Jenny. Akoni Raccoon envisioned a solid gold neck chain making him the most dashing figure on Yerba Buena Island. Amos Skunk was still thinking. Joaquin Hawk added that he would have his powerful claws fitted with golden tips that glistened in the sun as he cruised the airways over their island home. Jonathan Fox figured he would take his share back home and stash it. Finally, Owen Owl saw himself fitted with stylish gold-rimmed spectacles.

Then in unison, they asked, "What about you, Captain?"

"Oh, I don't know. I guess an old bleached skipper's hat with gold stitched embroidered wings on its bill would be fine for me." And then he added, "of course, I would wear it while leading this fearless crew aboard the Sitka on amazing journeys far beyond the seas."

As the crew cheered, Will interrupted them saying, "But first, we must find the gold." Everyone agreed; thus, the first gold search pondering session began.

They decided to divide into two teams, each taking a different route on either side of the river to search in trees, underwater, hills, caves and mountain terrain. Owen Owl would guide one team and Joaquin Hawk the other. Amos drew watch duty on the Sitka.

With nightfall bearing down, they retired to their usual niches around the roaring fireplace. Then, finally, they drifted off to sleep dreaming of gold. At that point, Mama asked, "And what will you dream about tonight, my son? Will you dream of gold, or will you dream of what Grandpa Liwanu will say tomorrow?" I knew that was a signal that story time was over for now, and it was time for dinner and then sleep. Grandpa looked a little worn anyway. Father helped steady him to his feet to walk home.

As I slept that night, the Sitka's Quest for Gold adventure danced in my head. As Mama thought, the lure of gold affected me a little too. Mama always knew what I was thinking, even before I did.

The following day, Grandpa Liwanu seemed anxious to get going with the story. So, we met at the tree at daybreak with blankets to keep warm. I have to say, it was fun hearing Grandpa describing how the morning sun cascaded heat and light throughout the region, drying out the mustiness. It was an ideal environment for prospecting. For an instant, it felt like we were in the story. I was excited to hear Grandpa say this new venture was just what the Sitka crew needed, and they were anxious to dig in. This new quest did sound a little dangerous, though. I hoped no one got hurt as Grandpa went on.

Armed with shovels, picks, and some tasty snacks for later, they were just about to leave when they ran into Lance and Terrance. "Where you all headed?" They asked, ears perked, raising their heads with a look of curiosity. Captain Will explained they were heading to the hills on a quest for gold and even invited them along.

Lance answered, "Can't. Have guard duty. But thanks anyway." Will's invitation seemed to put them at ease.

Then Terrance spoke up, "Better watch out for Miner Mike."

"Miner who?" asked Owen Owl.

"Miner Mike," repeated Terrance. "He's a crazy, hairy old miner living deep in the foothills who thinks he has a claim on all the gold up there."

"Shush," whispered Lance. "Remember, we're not supposed to talk about the wheat."

"Oh, right," said Terrance as he kept right on talking. "Well, he's cuckoo. He's been living in a one-room shack with that stupid mule of his, Ovie, as his only companion. I don't think he's too dangerous. He can't see that well but he does have an old musket or rifle. He may try to protect his imaginary claim though we don't recall him ever really finding any gold."

"Ixnay on the goldsnay," interrupted Lance again. "Okay! Okay! We stay clear of him. You should avoid him too. Not sure how he'd react to your bunch. Best of luck."

"Thanks for the heads up," replied Owen Owl, who then looked at Joaquin Hawk, commenting, "Did you catch all that?"

"Oh yeah," replied Joaquin, "another crazy human with a gun!"

Despite this warning from Lance and Terrance, the lure of gold beckoned the Sitka crew to the hills to seek their fortune. Once they arrived, Team One crossed an old bridge constructed decades before ago our forefathers. Then, they proceeded east up the north side of the river toward the hills leading to the mountains. Team Two headed up the south bank in the same direction toward Miner Mike's cabin among a smattering of small hills we call hillocks. This second team, comprised of Gio, Jenny, Gio Jr., and Jonathan Fox, were the fastest crew members and could execute a quick escape from Miner Mike if necessary. Joaquin Hawk joined them as a backup to attack from the sky if needed.

Team one had traveled a stretch when they decided to take a break and eat. While Sasha Beaver and Akoni Racoon sat down with their packed goodies from camp, Owen Owl was busy catching some tasty morsels from the trees and bushes. Captain Will was gobbling sugary honeycomb offerings he found while scratching his back against the scaly trunk of a aging redwood. For the moment, they had all lapsed in any thought of gold. Grandpa leaned over to chuckle in my ear that forest creatures can be easily distracted.

Then in his normal voice, he said on the other side of the river, Team Two had reached a rocky area sprinkled with boulders and some caves here and there. The river current jutted over rows of bedrock like a stepladder. In the distance, a little way up in a sparse area just off the beaten path was a small primitive dwelling constructed of old weathered wood planks with a tin roof and what hardly could be called a front porch. "That must be Miner Mike's place," Jenny whispered to Akoni. "Everyone be quiet, she cautioned, motioning with her right paw."

"I think Jenny Rabbit was a little nervous. So am I," whispered Grandpa. At this point, I was hanging onto his every word, squeezing Papa's arm so tight he had to pry open my fingers to loosen my grip. Grandpa went on to tell us, as they tried to sneak past the tiny shack, Joaquin Hawk, on a nearby tree branch, began squawking noisily and flapping his wings to warn them of something. But it was too late. They turned around and came face to face with Ovie, the mule. *One hee-haw out of him*, thought Jenny, *and we're all goners*. Luckily, for now, Ovie seemed perfectly content just staring at them while munching on some wild dandelions in their last cycle of life.

Now, family, it is common knowledge that mules are not known for their high IQs, * Grandpa. So I can tell you what Jonathan Fox was thinking, *Now what, that stupid mule makes one sound, Mad Mike comes out of the cabin, and we're toast*. In a moment of panic, he yanked a paw full of dandelions from the ground and tried to lure Ovie away from the cabin, and it was working at first. Then, suddenly, without warning, Ovie let out the ear-piercing braying sound mules are famous for. Right on cue, Miner Mike bolted out the cabin's front door, musket in hand, looking for intruders.

In this case, the first living thing he saw was Gio Rabbit, who did what rabbits typically do when suddenly faced with extreme, immediate danger. He froze in his tracks.

Father could not help but interrupt, "I've hunted many rabbits for their pelts and food over the years. I know firsthand that they do freeze when faced with danger making them easy targets, especially when distracted while eating. But I must say, I would think a rabbit that can talk, and reason would know to dart away when facing a human with a gun."

Grandpa Liwanu nodded in agreement. He explained that this was a defining moment for Gio, with his entire life flashing before him. Jonathan Fox dodged behind a boulder petrified, thinking he might be caught next. *I'm sure Gio's a goner; I'll run and get away, but Jenny and little Gio!* Breathing heavily, he mustered enough courage to hustle around the back of the cabin to rescue them on the other side of the porch, still in harm's way.

As he maneuvered, he heard that one horrible sound no animal ever wanted to hear, a gunshot. He slumped to his knees momentarily, thinking Gio was gone but quickly recovered, knowing Jenny and little Gio were still in grave danger. When he got to the other side of the cabin, to his complete shock and amazement, squatting there was not only Jenny and Jr. but also Gio Rabbit. Miner Mike had wandered off looking for the intruders.

On the opposite side of the porch whinnying with laughter, stood Ovie the mule. Jonathan Fox was perplexed and became even more baffled when Ovie looked right at him and spoke, "Well, that was a close one, huh? And by the way, I understood that stupid mule comment."

Jonathan apologized for that remark and asked Ovie, "What happened?"

While Ovie was educating Jonathan Fox on the other side of the river, Team one had reengaged their hunt for gold. High and low, they searched. In caves, on hilltops, along the shoreline, and being forest creatures, they even looked high up in trees but with no luck. "This gold sure is slippery," complained Akoni Racoon, wiping sweat from his brow. "No wonder the humans can't find it."

Of course, being simplistic forest creatures, their search targeted large gold rocks or stones. They failed to realize that precious, valuable objects can be small, slight, and subtle, just like some animals and people. Grandpa rubbed me on the top of my head before continuing. "On and on, they looked hopelessly. Would luck be on their side or destiny?" he said.

"Luck was certainly on Gio Rabbit's side," Ovie explained to Akoni. "You see, Miner Mike is nearly blind in one eye, and the other one's not much better. But you can't tell him that. He's looney as a jaybird. Can't find his shoes, let alone gold, but he keeps me fed and watered. And I try to keep him out of harm's way. It works. His aim is worse than his eyesight, so he never hits anything. I'm sure he's still looking for your rabbit friend. The fact is, he can't see anything unless it's moving right at him. Then, he still shoots three feet to the left."

"When I was Enyeto's age," Grandfather said, pointing at my father, "I could hit anything I aimed at with just a bow and arrow. Now, my eyes and my aim deceive me. Treasure your youth, hunter boy. Time belongs to the young and wisdom to the old. Now we leave the talking mule to see what he might say tomorrow."

Mother chimed in, "You hear that, Elsu?"

"I don't hear anything," I said.

"Just listen, Son, the talking mule says time for chores." I got the message and obeyed. I understood we all had a duty to the family, and I must carry my share. That was the Miwok way. But if I finished early, I could swim and play games with my friends. That was Elsu's way. Plus, I knew staying busy would keep me from wondering every minute what Grandpa might say tomorrow.

Thankfully, tomorrow did arrive, and so did Grandfather at the tree. "Family, I am well rested, but Captain Will and Team One, I tell you, they were withering from their search for gold." Tired and frustrated, Will looked for the right tree to relieve a nagging itch and help him relax. A few yards to his left, near a clump of rocks, was just the right one with rough, hardened bark in its last phase of life. So off Will marched, leaving the others to figure out the group's next move.

As he approached the tree, Will stumbled on some loose dirt and banged into it so hard it toppled over, exposing shallow roots due to soil erosion from harsh winters. Jonathan Fox and the others scurried over to check on their captain, who lay sprawled out on the ground just beyond the hole the tree had occupied moments before. Will was more than a little embarrassed. Nevertheless, everyone had a good chuckle over the mishap.

Of course, Lance and talkative Terrance had already leaked the news that the Sitka crew left on a quest for gold.

Captain John was concerned they might succeed as he'd granted them permission to harvest on his land before returning to Yerba Buena Island. So, he assembled a small band of his most trusted and fearless men armed with weapons and left in pursuit. They headed up the trail straight toward Miner Mike's place.

Father signaled to Grandpa he wished to make a point here. Grandpa acknowledged with a tilt of his head. "Elsu, this is an important part of Grandpa's story to learn about how some humans behave. We all have flaws, but Miwoks have always strived to be loyal to one another and considerate of outsiders. Sometimes in other cultures, loyalty is fleeting."

"What does fleeting mean, Papa?" I asked.

"In Grandpa's story, Captain John was loyal and faithful, even thankful to the Sitka crew for standing with his pet dogs against the coyotes. Yet, when something valuable like gold comes up, his loyalty is quickly replaced by greed and fear. It seems that gold was worth more than the lives of Terrane, Lance, and the Sitka crew members. He would even risk the lives of his men to possess something that did not belong to him but fed his greed and thirst for power."

John's worry was well founded. While he and his men were en route, Sasha Beaver, with keener eyesight due to his new spectacles from Captain John, spotted a shiny, yellowish sliver of something in the soil of the hole vacated by the tree Will knocked over. Akoni Racoon saw the glimmering substance too. Owen Owl, who had taken refuge in a heavily shaded tree nibbling on a catch, heard the commotion and swooped down to look. Now on his feet,

Will shook the dirt off and moved toward the other crew members to see for himself. He leaned over, grasped the small shiny flake piece in his paws, and held it to the sunlight.

"We're rich, we're rich," shouted Akoni, hopping up and down, his bushy ringed tail flailing excitedly.

"Let me see that," directed Owen Owl. Owen grabbed it with his stout beak, convinced the gold flake was genuine from its pliability. Then, with shovels in hand, the squad began digging feverishly, discovering the whole area around the hole was littered with the precious metal. They loaded sacks as full as they could carry and headed back down the hills toward the settlement.

Captain John and his men had just arrived at Miner Mike's cabin panting from their fast-paced search for the animals.

Sitka Team Two had experienced enough excitement for one day. They headed back to the settlement via a different route than Captain John, who was now pounding on Mike's door, yelling, "Mike, you get out here right now!" Pacing back and forth on the small porch, he bellowed, "I wanna talk to you about some trespassers."

Now, I'm sure to know that Miner Mike was not so crazy as to risk John's handouts. Humbly, he came out of his cabin, absent his musket, and explained what he knew about the group John was tracking. "I think I got one of um for you with my musket," he boasted, trying hard to impress his benefactor. "A fuzzy little critter with a brown foot. By the time I went inside to reload, they'd vamoosed," which was a big fib.

Captain John was disappointed to hear about Gio Rabbit but still fuming with concern the rest of the crew might find gold before him. He cautioned Mike, "Keep an eye out and fire a warning shot if you spot any of the others."

"You got it, Captain," responded Mike with a salute.

"I mean it, Mike. The first sign of any of them, you better let me know pronto, or else," John threatened as he angrily marched away.

Without so much as a blink of an eye, Miner Mike watched John leave while Ovie stood there blank-faced, occasionally bending down to munch on some vegetation.

Captain John and his men went further up the trail, then crossed a rickety old wooden bridge over a narrow part of the river to the other side. While backtracking, looking for Will and his crew, they stumbled across the toppled tree, gold still shimmering in the fresh dirt. It didn't take long for John to forget about Will, his crew, and the Sitka and focus on this historic discovery. *No one would believe a dumb group of animals, even talking ones, could make such an amazing find*, he reasoned.

In reality, once again, he owed Will a great debt of thanks. I couldn't help interrupting Grandpa again with my two cents, wondering, "But they're smart, talking animals who DID find the gold."

"Trust me, Elsu, talking animals are no match for talking humans." Father and Mother chuckled in agreement.

"Now, where was I? Oh yes," Grandpa said.

Both Sitka Teams made it back safely to the settlement, although Will's group took a little longer lugging those bags of gold. "This is a good time to head home," said Will. So quickly, they loaded up the boat with supplies, food crops, and, of course, the gold, then shoved off bound for their precious island home. All seemed well at first, but then mechanical problems stalled the return trip. To everyone's dismay, they were forced to re-dock the Sitka.

With the return trip now sidetracked and lacking any mechanical skills, the group settled in for an early lunch to figure out their next move. However, a fascinating conversation centering on Gio Rabbit unfolded, leading to unthinkable intrigue and discovery and changing the very fabric of their expedition.

"Maybe we should stop here and continue tomorrow," said Grandpa, sensing I was dying to know what happened next.

Then, a familiar voice from the village area yelled, "Elsu, Elsu, come swim with me. Whatcha doin'?" It was Kono, my best friend from the far side of our village. "C'mon, let's go," he insisted. Now, swimming and horsing around with Kono was very tempting but not as much as finding out what happened next to the Sitka crew. I pleaded with Grandpa for Kono to join us to hear more of the story. Finally, Grandpa conceded to keep going waving Kono to sit with us under the tree. He seemed pleased to have another young listener.

"Ok, listen," said Grandpa. "There's going to be some twists and turns in this next part of the story, so no interruptions," looking squarely at me as my parents looked away, smiling.

Chapter 4
Gio's Bright Cave

While the crew ate, Captain Will shifted close to Gio to ask, "How did you know to find us just in time for that battle in the pastures? I know Calvin was sure surprised to see you." Gio thought for a minute, then replied, "I remember being very angry, wandering the foothills looking for Warrick Wolf and getting lost. I must have searched for hours. I started feeling tired and found this nice airy cave to lay down for a spell. I remember closing my eyes to take a nap but after a short while, my ears began tingling, and I started getting these strange, hazy images. As they became clearer, I could see our island home, us aboard the Sitka, and that guard dog chasing me when I fell in the hole. Next, I could see little Gio and Jenny and then some far-off place with many boats and people. Then, suddenly, as clear as day, I saw the battle with the coyotes, Warrick standing by your side, then Lance and Terrance going after Calvin."

"I was sure I was dreaming, but it was all so clear and bright. When I saw Jenny and Jr. in harm's way, without even thinking, out of that cave, I bolted down the hills straight to the pastures."

"Rabbits are famous for bolting without thinking," Grandpa added.

Then, Gio continued, "Next thing I knew, I was right in the middle of the fight, as if right on cue. That's all I remember, except as I arrived, I thought, *why is Warrick standing there with Captain Will against the coyotes and dogs*? So, I figured I would join the fight with you and the crew and deal with Warrick later."

"Now that's quite a story," said Owen Owl. "You know, sometimes when I'm high up in a tree late at night with the moon and stars shining bright, I see strange images too."

Gio corrected Owen, "No, it wasn't like that at all. The whole cave suddenly lit up. It got really bright. Then I left. I didn't have time to look around once I saw my wife and son in danger."

"That's very odd and curious," commented Akoni Fox.

"Yeah," chimed in Jenny, her eyebrows arched, glaring in Will's direction. "Curious enough to investigate?"

In one voice, the crew shouted, "Yes!" Because what could be stranger and weirder than a brightly lit cave as if by magic? After polishing off dinner, they settled in for a good night's sleep to try fixing the Sitka's mechanical issues in the morning. Because if they couldn't, they'd be forced to ask Captain John for Harper's help, something they hoped to avoid. And then, there was the matter of how to find Gio's bright cave.

Everyone slept well that night. That is, everyone except Captain Will. In the quiet, as he scratched his back against the Sitka's mast, Will wondered and imagined. Again, he was haunted by that recollection of a journey across the sea on that schooner many years ago. But where had he come from and why. These thoughts tormented him endlessly. A puzzle he couldn't seem to solve no matter how long and hard he pondered or scratched.

Morning came drafty blue, stirring the crew with the sweet aroma of Sasha's mint tea. Following some yawning and stretching, Will summoned everyone to the mast to check out the Sitka's mechanical problem and discuss how they might find Gio's bright cave. As it turned out, Jonathan Fox noticed that a bolt connecting the cylinder rod to the paddlewheel crankshaft was loose, causing a shimmy that was easy to fix. Finding Gio's cave, not so easy.

Aside from the fact that Gio didn't know which one he'd been in, caves of all sizes and shapes zigzagged across the foothills, a real puzzle. But this courageous group would not give up easily.

"Owen, give us your most expert thinking on this riddle," asked Captain Will.

Owen's eyes arched with razor-sharp focus as he began to think, and think, and think some more. But alas, to no avail. "Perplexing," said Owen, "most vexing. *But how do I unvex the vexed*," he muttered to himself, *hmm.*

Then an idea struck him. "Perhaps if I fly to one of the tallest tree limbs where the air is purer, the extra oxygen might help me think better." So, up Owen flew to the sturdiest branch in the highest redwood he could find. He could see all the way to the beautiful lagoon. He marveled at the cascading waterfall guarded by majestic pines. Silver lupine and multi-color buttercups seemed to bloom right out of moss-covered boulders. At this oxygen-rich height shaded nicely by the canopy of treetops, Owen began to think. That is until he was interrupted by a loud squawking sound that nearly startled him off his perch.

Owen turned toward the direction of the obnoxious noise. He was stunned to see sitting on a branch just opposite his a large, exotic-looking bird with more colors than wildflowers blooming in spring. He had an oversized hook-shaped beak that seemed larger than the rest of him and was staring straight at Owen. "Where'd you come from?" asked Owen, slightly annoyed.

"Well, I could ask you the same question, but I already know. I've been watching you and that band of misfits for hours aboard that little dingy down there."

This bird is a real character, Owen thought, *but he might know the area. Maybe he'll tell us something useful if I cozy up to him.*

"Forgive me. Where are my manners? My name is Owen, Owen Owl. I'm from a faraway place called Yerba Buena. My comrades and I are here on a great quest for gooolarticfacts to show our family and friends back on our island home."

"Looks like Owen almost spilled the beans about the gold," Kono said, laughing.

"Yes," replied Grandpa. "Secrets are hard to keep, especially about gold as he returned to finish Owen's bird-on-bird conversation."

"And may I again ask who you are?"

"My name is Morgan, Morgan McCaw. I live near the lagoon over yonder."

Morgan flew over to the branch where Owen was perched and continued their chat. "Yeah, I like watching others, you know, eavesdropping. Never know what someone will say, ark, what they will say. I really like watching humans glancing toward Captain John's compound. It keeps me from being bored since they're always yakking about things they shouldn't be yakking about. I eavesdrop on them a lot. Just the other day, I heard them whispering about magic wheat (ark), magic wheat. They were trying to be sneaky. Everyone knows that's code word for nugget. Heck, everyone's been looking for that thing forever."

"Well," Owen confided, "We did find a little gold, and then we—"

Morgan cut off Owen mid-sentence, "Not that gold, not that gold, magic nugget, magic nugget." Then, lowering his voice, Morgan whispered, "Very special powers. Talk to Mike, aark, talk to Mike. He knows. Everyone knows you know."

Morgan's comment about the nugget suddenly reminded Owen why he was in the tree in the first place. Now he was connecting the dots. *Could this nugget Morgan speaks of be connected to the cave? Maybe it's in the cave. I must tell the others right away but first, what about Morgan? Hmmm,* Owen thought. *A parrot spy might be handy on a quest, and it would add another flyer.*

So, pending an aye vote from the crew, Owen invited Morgan to join them on their adventure aboard the Sitka. Off they flew to make the formal introductions.

Meanwhile, as Morgan had claimed, Captain John and his men at that very moment were combing through the gold hoard first discovered by Captain Will at the tree stump. On his knees, John dug frantically, yelling at his men, "Get back, out of the way. It's mine." Hour after hour, Captain

John clawed the dirt recklessly, scavenging the area looking for the mystical treasure as his men looked on from a distance.

As dusk approached and John was about to abandon the search, something in the soil about twelve paces above the stump hole caught his eye. It was an odd-shaped stone that seemed to be illuminating, or maybe it was just the dwindling light from the sun at dusk. Englishman Harper commented, "whoa, that surely is a grand piece. Never seen the likes of that before. I salute you, Captain."

But John heard nary a word. Shoving some of his men out of the way, he pounced on the find, inspecting it repeatedly in the little natural light that remained. "This has to be it," he exclaimed. "It must be. Finally, after all these years (hands together in a prayerful clasp)."

Unbeknownst to them, eyes were watching from the nearby trees and brush to the left and the hills overlooking the area. But John and his men were too busy gauging the magnificent find in the now colorless hue of darkness. They never noticed Warrick Wolf lying silent and still between some boulders above them, gazing down on all the commotion. With his keen sight and smell, Warrick sensed something else downwind from John and his men. A familiar scent that made the hair on the back of his neck stand up. Coyotes.

That meant just one thing to Warrick. Calvin had survived the crop fields skirmish, and he and his mangy pack were up to no good. Also, judging from the rowdy hoopla by Captain John and his men, they found the special nugget, and Calvin probably knew that too. Ever so slowly,

Warrick eased from his hiding place and returned to his cave to think.

Owen and Morgan had just landed on the Sitka, causing quite a stir with two flyers instead of one. Captain Will thought the second bird was a predator chasing Owen. So, he let out a ferocious growl moving toward the bow that nearly caused both birds to miss the tea kettle, their landing target. "Easy, easy," yelled Owen. "Everyone, calm down. He's with me."

"And he being who?" asked Akoni Raccoon.

At that, Morgan spoke up, "Good day to you, sirs and madam rabbit. I am Morgan, Morgan McCaw of the lagoon McCaws by way of St. Lucia. Quoi de neuf?"

Now Sasha Beaver didn't understand this comment, thinking it was an insult. "Hey, what did you call me?" he questioned, aggressively striking his powerful tail on the deck. "What was that?"

"Whoa, calm down, Sasha," Will intervened. "He just asked, what's up? That's all."

At that point, Jenny Rabbit interrupted, "Pardon me for butting in, Sasha, but Captain, since when do you understand French? 'Cause that sure sounded like some French I heard from humans on the far side of Yerba Buena Island."

"I don't know," Will responded hesitantly, scratching his head. With that, Morgan reeled off a string of questions in French at Captain Will:

How did you come to be associated with this group of amateurs (alors comment estes-vous venu a ester associe a group)? I've known this group of amateurs most of my life;

they are my dearest friends (eh bien, j ai connu ces beaux comrads la plupart de ma vie).

Where is Yerba Buena Island (ou est Yerba Buena Island)? Our island home is slightly northwest of here, where the river funnels into the great bay (Notre maison de l ile est au mord-est d ici ou la riviere se deverse dans la grande baie).

Are there any McCaws there (Y a t il des MaCaws)? I've never seen any there but there might be (Je n ai jamais vu de MaCaw sur l ile mais ils pourraient etre la).

Can I come visit (Puis-je venir visiter)? We'd be honored if you visited (Nous sevions honor essi vous quez visite). There would be a spot right next to the campfire just for you to share some of your amazing stories (Il y aura un endroit special au few de camp qui vous attend).

"Excuse me, Grandfather Liwanu, but do you speak French?" asked Kono.

Grandpa turned to answer Kono directly. "Miwoks and other tribes learned some French and Spanish from foreign explorers," he explained. "But to answer your question, young one, no, I cannot speak French." Then, he continued with the story, leaving Kono with a confused look.

I leaned over and whispered, "Don't worry, Kono, I'll explain later," as Grandpa continued.

While that surprising foreign language exchange was happening, a much different conversation occurred in the depths of Coyoteville. This secluded forest region somewhere beyond the lagoon area and above the northwest border of Captain John's property was a mecca for the coyote population.

Standing on a rocky ledge in the heart of Coyoteville, Calvin was addressing his clan of family and loyalists. "Brethren, we yield from a long unbroken line of hunters. Our ancestors founded this land as far as the eye can see. They founded and yes, died to protect our legacy. This land represents our heritage, our birthright. And look at us now, vanquished to scratching out a meager existence on this pitiful parcel of nothing. Once, we were the rulers of this kingdom, and all inhabitants therein called us Lords. We have become weak and humiliated. We have no pride, honor, or sense of purpose anymore. But I say to you this day; we can restore our greatness and reclaim our heritage."

"Our forsaken kin long past can once again look down on us with pride that we have achieved victory over our enemies who shackled and reduced us to this shameful state. We need but control our own destiny, and today I offer you a path forward, a new future where coyotes resume their rightful place."

"Our ancestors often spoke of a particular stone. But not just any stone; a nugget wielding inexplicable power beyond the imagination. An element from our own homeland that rightfully belongs to us. A stone that can end our plight and restore us to our rightful standing." Raising his right paw as a fist he shouted, "we only have to reclaim it from the humans who invaded and conquered our sacred domain. Are you prepared to reclaim your heritage? If your answer is yes, then I say to you, a simple piece of earth, a small pebble holds the key to our salvation."

(Following a long pause for effect) "I stand before you today, ready to lead this quest. Are you with me?"

Unanimously, the clan roared a hail, "Calvin! Hail Coyoteville!"

I have them now, Calvin confided to himself, *total allegiance*. Or was it? For rarely is anything one hundred percent certain, even among animals—especially cunning, cliquish coyotes.

Father interrupted to comment that Coyoteville was but small version of human society where power often rules and corrupts while some cultures are treated poorly.

Then Grandpa went on to explain that Coyoteville was no different, and Calvin keenly grasped this concept. He and his family stumbled upon this refuge where the founder clans had long lived in peace and harmony, unbothered by outside influence or internal strife. They would board a lost or injured stranger from time to time who would integrate into their society, embracing their customs and way of life. All for one and one for all, respect the elders.

That is, until Calvin and his misfits arrived. Carefully, they integrated and maneuvered their rise to power developing a cult following while weakening the true coyote tribe that initially settled Coyoteville. Now, he would elevate himself to elite status at their expense with slick speeches and hollow promises.

But not everyone was on board with Calvin's plan. Not everyone was as gullible as Calvin thought or hoped.

While this undercurrent simmered, the otherwise serene Coyoteville continued with typical daily activities. Pups played and skirmished without distinction. The bowl-like mezzanine design of Coyoteville was ideal for hollowing out dens for moms to bear pups which explained the growing population.

Males usually hunted near or on Captain John's property or perched on the perimeter hilltops, noses to the air, sniffing and surveying for threats. The deepest part of the bowl functioned as a basin with its own microclimate storing rainwater and serving as a community hub. There, elders would gather from their lower-level dens under green canopies to reminisce about long-forgotten battles won and lost against humans. The deep bowl layout housing the elders' quarters and water pools maintained a steady, comfortable temperature year-round several degrees lower than the ridge. Thick, thorny brush, dense trees, and the steep terrain outside the bowl rendered Coyoteville virtually invisible and inaccessible to humans.

While life flourished, that undercurrent thrived too. A growing sentiment to oust Calvin and his rogue followers echoed throughout many dens. Mutiny was afoot.

Grandpa cupped his hands to whisper, "So, the stage was set. As it turns out, the secret of the magical nugget was no secret at all. And as we all know, secrets are tough to keep secret. But how many know the same secret? Only time will tell. And that time wasn't far off."

Then using his regular voice, Grandpa resumed saying, "How far off no one knew. But I can tell you this family, everyone wanted that precious artifact for themselves but for different reasons. Captain John sought absolute power over all that is. Calvin desired control over the region and revenge for past grievances. Poor Warrick hoped its power might restore life to his fallen family. And the Sitka crew weren't exactly sure what they were dealing with. Secretively though, Will hoped that maybe, just maybe, if the stone was real, it might bring him long-sought answers about his past."

At least, Owen finally solved how to find Gio's bright cave. "Gio, didn't you say your ears tingled when the cave got bright?" asked Owen.

"Yeah," chimed in Amos Skunk, even before Gio could speak. "Sometimes my tail tingles right before I, uh, sorry, go on, Owen."

Owen looked sternly at Amos, "We just need to get Gio over to those caves and see which one makes his ears tingle."

The whole crew liked Owen's plan except for Joaquin Hawk, frowning with a question. "And how do you propose we get him over there? Let me guess, fly him on my back."

"Correct," stated Owen.

"Well, he's not as light as he looks," complained Joaquin.

"Mm," mumbled Owen. "Well, what about Gio Jr.? He's light enough and has his father's ears." Of course, Jenny Rabbit scoffed at that idea but relented since they were now racing against the possibility of some other group locating the cave first.

"So, that's settled," confirmed Owen. "Gio Jr. will ride on Joaquin's back while Morgan and I fly shotgun. Once we land and find the right cave, we'll signal the rest of you. Morgan, can you do the signal?"

"Sure, a shrill should do the trick."

"What's that sound like?" asked Will.

"Don't worry," chuckled Morgan, "you'll know when you hear it."

Since the day was nearly gone, the crew with Morgan decided to relax on the deck of the Sitka. Sasha and Akoni took their turn preparing dinner. The evening was beautifully tranquil, with the stars glowing so bright it nearly seemed like day.

"Magnificent, aren't they," Owen commented to Morgan. He continued boasting, "You know, I'm a highly respected authority on astronomy, particularly star signs. I've studied constellations most of my life. Did you know there is a small one up there called Apus for Bird of Paradise, like yourself? I think you can see it best during summer, around July."

"Aark!" Retorted Morgan. "I have my own star?"

At that point, the rest of the crew talked about their stars simultaneously. Even Captain Will made a snide remark about Bootes, aiming a sly grin Owen's way. Owen whispered in Morgan's ear softly as he could, "I wouldn't mention anything to the captain about his star. He's quite touchy about that."

"Touchy, touchy," squawked Morgan.

"Shh, you're gonna get me in a lot of trouble," whispered Owen. So, Morgan, being the newcomer, wisely shut his beak, at least for the time being. But it is well-known that parrots are famous for saying or repeating things at the wrong time.

As everyone settled into familiar spots along the deck, some intense stargazing commenced with Owen, astronomer extraordinaire, offering his expert opinion here and there.

Lucky for Owen, Will retired early, anticipating an eventful tomorrow. Finally, as the rest of the crew drifted off to sleep, Owen and Morgan kept watch through the night in a nearby tree, reliving past eavesdropping escapades by Morgan.

Mother added, "While the women are working hard all day hulling, seeding, leeching, and grinding acorns, I can't help but overhear their remarks and conversations. Of course, I'm sure they listen to me too. So, I guess that is kind of like eavesdropping."

Father mildly scoffed under his breath at that. Good thing Mother did not hear him. Grandpa looked a little annoyed by the interruption.

We quieted down as Grandpa went on to say that humans need little reason to celebrate anything. So, of course, a wild party honoring Captain John's historical find was in process at the settlement. While his men were busy weighing the gold hoard, bragging about how to spend it, John examined the rare nugget, trying to figure out how its magic worked. *Odd-shaped thing*, he thought. *Kinda resembles a bear. I wonder if some strange chant about a bear makes it work. I must figure this out*, he surmised while downing another pint.

"Maybe if you rub it, it'll grant you three wishes," chided Harper.

"Oh, come now, Captain, live a little. You're bloomin' rich now. That darn nugget isn't going anywhere." John finally tore himself away from the rock and obliged by having yet another pint. Later, everyone passed out in a drunken stupor, everyone except John.

Chapter 5
The Great Heist

In Coyoteville, Calvin secretly organized a small troop of ninja coyotes to steal the magic stone right from under Captain John's nose. Warrick Wolf devised his own plan to loot the precious rock. "I must get that nugget before Calvin does or the humans figure out how to unlock its magic. Tonight's the night. I must try, for my family's sake," as he slumped down on the floor of his cave, tearfully recalling happier times, their images seared in his memory.

Captain John was still puzzled by the bear-shaped object trying every trick he could think of to unleash its power. Since he found it near a tree stump hole, it never dawned on him that a cave might be part of the equation to conjure up its magic. So, he was at a dead end without knowing it.

As night descended, John, weary of trying to crack the stone's code, left the great room and slipped off to bed but not before hiding it under a floorboard. Then he shoved one of his bed legs over it for good measure. *There, that should do it,* he muttered, dozing off to sleep where his dreams of power and fame consumed him.

Standing on the third-floor balcony of his colonial mansion at daybreak, Sir John gazed upon his imaginary estate. The backdrop charade of manicured grounds, expansive grove of native oaks, and beautiful rose garden gave him an undeniable feeling of superiority. Perfectly trimmed hedges bordered a spacious courtyard hosting an exquisitely tiled but overstated coy pond featuring swans spewing water streams ten feet high. And all, shamefully constructed and maintained by indentured workers.

Sir John barked out the day's orders to his legion of minions as house servants awaited instructions for his breakfast meal. *I am master here,* he confided to himself, smiling ear to ear. "Take a letter, Sarah," he commanded, raising his right hand fittingly with a mint julep in his left.

"Yes, my lord," she responded with a curtsy.

Esteemed Governor Sloke,

Please be informed of my pending arrival at the Presidio this twelfth of June, 1600 hours. I petition a meeting to address renegade intrusion activity off the west corridor of my territory. Furthermore, I beseech assignment of a garrison to suppress said nuisance. Likewise, I seek your endorsement acquiring a land tract situated in Yerba Buena proper. Said acquisition should be most favorable, if not profitable, to our mutual business aspirations. I arrive by launch and am available to dine at your leisure. Till then,

Best Regards,
Sir John Miller, esquire.

While Captain John played ruler of his fairytale kingdom in dreamland, Calvin and his ninjas, clad in black with masks to match, were on their way to relieve him of the treasure. By coincidence, Warrick, also dressed in black, sneaked down the mountainside with the same idea.

The tension was thick as tule fog occasionally hanging in low patches over the region, creating the perfect backdrop for a heist.

"What a story," hollered Kono.

Mother added, "Yes, it's a great story that Grandfather will pick up tomorrow afternoon. It's almost dinner time, and he needs to rest. Elsu, please walk Kono back to the village. Then come eat."

"Yes, Mother," I answered.

Kono and I headed toward the main village about halfway to his family's hut frolicking all the way. Then Kono asked, "Oh yeah, how can your grandfather speak French, then say he doesn't speak French?" So, I explained the whole story to Kono leading up to today, including the part about Hanta and the brown bear cub and the connection between it and my forefathers. "Boy, I can't wait to get home and tell my parents. Can I bring them tomorrow to listen? Please?"

"I'm sure Grandpa won't mind," I said.

As Kono scampered the rest of the way home, I returned to mine feeling a little taller, knowing that now, I had a role in telling the Sitka story. But then, it dawned on me. Someday this incredible story or tale will be mine to pass on.

When I got home, Mother had dinner waiting. After giving thanks, we ate. As I raised another spoonful to my mouth, I could not help staring at Grandfather Liwanu. His wrinkled face, hands, and slow movements made me wonder how much time he had left. Then, for whatever reason, I thought about the bear that laid her fish at his feet. And I remembered Grandpa saying that in time I would understand. But at ten years old, my curiosity was getting the better of me.

Father noticed my silence and asked, "Are you okay, my son?"

"Yes, Father, just thinking about how life is."

"Don't overthink that, Elsu. Ten-year-olds should be thinking about fishing and hunting."

"And chores," added Mother.

"Life will come as it will come," said Father. "Now, we all can use a good night's sleep."

"Yes, I have acorns in the morning, and Father has business in the village. I think it is also wash day," Mama mentioned as a subtle message. "Help Grandpa to his room."

"Yes, Mama. Come, Grandpa," as I held him by the arm to steady him. Once Grandpa settled into his several layers of tule reed mats and animal skins, I went to bed to do the same.

Before falling asleep, I lay there for a while playing with wooden figures of some of the Sitka crew Father carved for me. I imagined cruising down the river on the Sitka steamboat with Captain Will at the rudder, and Joaquin Hawk perched on the kettle. As I drifted off to sleep, the crew's images danced in my dreams.

The faint smell of lavender from Grandfather Liwanu's room the following day helped me awaken. You see,

Grandpa was old but first to sleep, first to rise. Plus, our rooms were just different areas of a huge tule hut separated by a fireplace in the middle surrounded by stones. Father would place animal skin over the smoke hole when it rained to keep the water out. The sound of a million pebbles hitting the roof signaled a light rain the next morning, so Father covered the hole. But a little rain does not stop Miwoks from tending to their duties.

Mother was already gone to the village to work the acorns. Father left again to gather firewood and harvest wild berries from the bramble bushes before heavier rain and cold damaged them too much. Strawberries hate drenched soil, and blueberries dislike the cold. This day was both so best to harvest before any fungus set in. I felt sorry for Mama having to work the acorns in a drizzling rain, so I did the wash without being told. I also cleaned all the eating bowls and spoons and tidied up the whole hut. I was anxious for Father and Mother to return to see what a good helper I was beyond my regular chores.

Grandfather Liwanu sat outside the hut, wrapped in a deerskin hide under a tree shielded from the rain smoking his pipe. Sometimes he would chuckle or talk to himself for no reason at all. At times, I thought he talked to my grandma Papina. Today I figured he was just anxious about story time at the tree. So was I.

Everyone was busy till midafternoon. Then, as if by magic, the sun peeked through, pushing the clouds apart and drying out the dampness. I got excited, figuring story time was definitely on. Grandpa had gone inside earlier to nap after nibbling on some leftover smoked fish and acorn mash. I think he, too, was excited about the next part of the story.

As late afternoon approached, Kono, his parents, and several other kids with their parents showed up. I ran over to the tree to secure our regular spots. The others found seats as close to us as they could. I was starting to feel like one of the characters in the story, and I really liked that.

I sensed that interruptions this afternoon would not be welcome cause Grandpa had much to tell. Lately, he seemed to be straining to get more and more of the story out. That caused me to again wonder how much time Grandpa had left.

Even at ten, I understood that death comes to everyone sooner or later. I witnessed some of our warriors dying from battle wounds, which was difficult. On hunts, I participated in the killing of animals for food. Death was a part of Miwok's life. When I looked at Grandpa Liwanu, I felt joy that our ancestral spirits had blessed him with old age and me with the years I was getting to spend with him.

Grandpa, Mama, and Father made their way over to the tree and sat in the spots I saved for them. Then, as I wiggled my butt to make a more comfortable pocket in the pine needles, Grandpa began.

"Now, let's see, yesterday I left off with the coyotes and Warrick Wolf plotting to steal the magic stone from Captain John. Yes, that's right. The coyotes arrived at his house first. They hid in the trees just beyond the entrance, where they could canvass the area without detection. Their black garb blending with the low-hanging fog made them near invisible."

Warrick was still en route, mindful of his self-imposed duty to his family, driving him to risk his own life to reclaim theirs. This courageous yet petrified wolf was driven by fear and longing.

As Calvin, his chief ninja thief Okami and crew slithered toward John's front porch, Warrick had just arrived at the back, panting heavily with anticipation. *Ok, first things first, where are Terrance and Lance? Hmmm, no sign of 'em. Maybe they're inside. Why am I talking to myself? It's just me here.* Little did he know that since the great battle in the crop field, the guard dogs were assigned to the barn to monitor the crop fields full-time. So, they were nowhere close to the main house but still within earshot.

Warrick had never been this close to the human settlement before. He was more than a little nervous and confused by the new smells. Unfortunately, the scent of coyotes got lost in the equation. Cautiously, he eased his way to the back window and peeked in with only the faintest shimmer of moonlight, mixing with the fog to cast eerie shadows. Warrick could barely see anything, but his keen wolf ears picked up snoring so loud the walls shook.

As luck would have it, he was staring right into Captain John's bedroom window. Using one of his knife-like nails, he carefully shifted the lock open. Then, with a faint click, he nudged the window to gain entry. Once inside, he thoroughly combed the room searching for the artifact as John snored on, the nugget stashed safely beneath the floorboard. *Hmmm, not here. Maybe it's in another room,* thought Warrick.

He left the bedroom and sneaked past the crew's quarters toward the great hall. Okami tiptoed around the side of the house to the back and slid into John's bedroom via the same window just used by Warrick. Okami froze as Captain John shifted slightly, locating a soft, warm crease on his mattress. Then, after a few, nasally snorts resumed his loud snoring.

"Good Lord," muttered Okami. "He sounds like a big old grizzly." Unworried about John's awakening, Okami thoroughly searched the bedroom, finding nothing. Then, as he crept back to the window to leave, he stepped close to one of the legs of the bed and heard what sounded like a hollow creak. *I wonder*, Okami thought.

He went out the window and around the side of the house to find Calvin and the others. By this time, they'd managed to pick the front door lock and were now spreading out in the great hall to search.

As Warrick was about to enter, he spotted his treacherous enemies. Grossly outnumbered, he retreated a few paces to avoid detection and think, and think quickly he did. *I'll pull my mask down tightly to disguise my face. I hope this works.* Then, immersed in black clothing, he blended in with the coyotes who were so focused on searching for the nugget that none of them noticed Warrick, who was now mimicking their movements.

So far, so good, he thought. Captain John's men, sleeping through their stupor from the night before, wouldn't know a coyote from a goat. After a fruitless search, Calvin commanded his troops to vacate the premises. Warrick purposely lagged behind as the last one out to make his escape. Once outside, they ran into Okami, who signaled for Calvin to come over as Warrick slipped into the dark, patchy night.

"I think I know where the nugget is," whispered Okami.

"Good, good," said Calvin. "Just follow my lead."

As a dejected Warrick returned to his cave, Calvin called the other coyotes to a clearing just beyond the edge of the woods. "My brave warriors, I know you may be disappointed we failed to achieve our goal tonight but fear not. I know we are close to our objective, for I could feel the nugget beckon to me. I will take Okami and return to the cabin to fulfill our mission. Return to Coyoteville and rouse everyone to prepare for a great victory celebration. We will prevail. Now, go!"

As the now hopeful coyotes left for home, Calvin and Okami tiptoed around the back of the cabin, where Okami explained the hollow sound on the floor. A clever Calvin reasoned that since the structure had a porch, there must be a subfloor, a perfect hiding place for something valuable. They checked the perimeter outside Captain John's bedroom and found some loose planks they could pry off. In they went.

It was darker than dark under the house and a virtual dust bowl. Calvin and Okami crawled around dragging on their bellies due to the tight space, occasionally nicking themselves on debris.

Clank! "Did you hear that?" whispered Okami.

"Hold on," responded Calvin as he maneuvered his left paw to his side, where he felt the edge of something sharp. He tried to look, but it was too dark and dingy to see. With insufficient space to turn his body, Calvin strained to feel its surface to ensure it wasn't a rock or stick or something.

The edge was straight. Moving his paw a little further, he felt a sharp point like a corner. "I've got something," whispered Calvin. "Let's get out of here." They backed out and scampered into the woods to inspect what they found.

"This might be it," shouted Calvin. It was a small black box with engraving on the lid and a keyhole, meaning it was probably locked.

"How do we open it?" Okami asked.

"A key, a key," I shouted, trying to insert myself into the story and drawing a stern look from Grandpa as he went on.

"No time for that now," retorted Calvin. "Let's go." Energized, they ran full tilt through the forest to Coyoteville with Okami in the lead, the box tucked firmly in Calvin's jaw.

A rude, eventful morning unknowingly awaited Captain John as the night belonged to Calvin. However, while he and Okami were en route, something unexpected occurred in Coyoteville.

Calvin's troops had returned and ordered the village to prepare for the celebration as instructed. But a small group of rebels was resistant. They had questioned Calvin's motives and even his heritage from the very start. This underground insurrection brewing for some time finally reached its boiling point.

In Calvin's absence, the leader of this coup seized the opportunity to squash Calvin's plans. He'd already convinced most of the villagers that Calvin was not even of pure blood, that he was a descendant of mutt coyote outsiders who infiltrated the pack during better times. For proof, he offered distinctions and variations between the pure bloods and Calvin and his followers; powerful dignified curvature of the tail, stout chest, straight erect ears, and deep Mediterranean-colored fur.

Calvin had none of these features. Plus, his fur was a tangled, patchy dirty tan.

Proclaiming himself as their commander was the last straw. That was not the coyote way. Soon as Calvin returns, they would take the artifact from him and use its magnificent power to uplift the authentic coyote society from its meager existence. It seems as if Calvin is in for something rude and eventful too.

Morning came with sunlight piercing Captain John's bedroom window coaxing him out of bed. A stretch here, a yawn there as he slipped into his robe and slippers to enjoy a splendid day knowing his valuable little gem was tucked safely away.

Let's see how Harper and those drunken misfits are doing this morning, he chuckled. He rang the large bell in the great hall signaling time for breakfast, but all he heard were moans and groans from every room. "Parlay," yelled Harper as if he was on some vessel at sea. "Grant us sreep, I replore you."

Best leave them to sleep for a while longer, murmured John. *I'll just go polish up my little gem and see if I can get it to work.*

Imagine his anger and dismay when he reached under the floorboard to an empty cavity. "*Noooo*, it must be here," he cried out. Still, in his robe and slippers, John bolted out the front door and around the side of the cabin. When he got to the corner of his bedroom, he saw some boards sealing the subfloor were pried off. Spewing profanities, John dove on the ground and crawled beneath his bedroom, heart racing, oblivious to the dirt, grime, and spider webs. He kept feeling around for the case grasping only a rock or stick here and there. Then he felt something fuzzy, something familiar.

He backed out of the space furious, stood up, and shook off all the dirt and grime as best he could. His robe was covered in strands of brownish clinging fur. "Coyotes," he exclaimed, "those no-good thieving coyotes."

Sensing that Grandfather might need a minute to rest; Father asked if he needed a break. Grandpa took a second to scan the group. Then, seeing they were totally absorbed in the story, he waved off Father (a familiar motion), saying, "I'm fine, Enyeto."

He resumed saying that Captain John yelled to his men, "Get dressed and meet me on the front porch. Looks like we'll be having coyote for breakfast today, boys." Grandpa smirked a little at that before continuing.

Morning at Coyoteville offered quite a different scenario playing out. First, Calvin was discarded as the leader and relieved of the black box. Then he was banished from the village along with his loyal mutt cronies. However, Calvin did manage to accomplish one thing before leaving. The victory celebration he ordered would go on as scheduled, just without him. Later that night, the order of Coyoteville would unleash the magic of the nugget for their unknown purpose.

Chapter 6
Magic or Myth

Beyond the foothills, a cheerier proposition was unfolding.

The Sitka flyers had just landed with Gio Jr. to search for his dad's bright cave. Their flight took them over breathtaking vistas of thick green forests dominated by tall pines and humming with life. Wooded areas separated expansive meadows with sheep and goats grazing on yummy thick wild grass. Wild pansies, peonies, and bright yellow buttercups portraying joy, youth, purity, happiness, and friendships, all pillars of Miwok society blanketed rolling fields. They saw sparkling waterways servicing local animal life and marveled at the hills and mountains dotted with caves and caverns of all sizes. Moss-covered boulders seemingly sprouted plants from their centers.

"This is exciting," shouted Jr., his furry little tail twitching faster than a humming bird's wings. This time, the expedition's success rested not on Captain Will, or Sasha Beaver, or Owen, or even his pop, but on his sturdy little shoulders. "Was he ready?" kidded Grandpa, glancing around at the kids giggling with anticipation.

Ears erect and eyes focused, Jr. hopped down the path flanked by Morgan, Owen, and Joaquin. Slowly, he entered cave one and squatted very still. *Hmmm, no tingling here,* he said to himself. So out of the cave, he came to tell the others waiting with hopeful looks on their faces, "Sorry, nothing in that one."

"That's okay," assured Owen. "There are lots of caves to look in. I'm sure we'll find the right one." All the flyers encouraged Jr. that he would find his dad's bright cave if they kept looking.

Further down the path, he circled some bushes when he came to cave two. It was larger and angled a little more from the direct sun, making it darker inside than the first one. Collecting his courage, in he went. It was also much deeper than the first cave, so he thought maybe this was the one. He advanced far enough to see the rear wall and squatted down to concentrate.

After a few minutes, absent any tingling, he left and continued down the trail arriving at cave three, thinking, *I've got to find dad's cave; he's depending on me. Please be the one.* Gio Jr. entered, finding this cave brighter than the other two and very comfortable and airy. Feeling a little more hopeful, he squatted down again, and although he sensed a strange feeling about this cave, his ears failed to tingle at all.

Off he went, squatting in cave after cave after cave with no luck.

Dejected and about to give up, he noticed one last cave tucked around the corner of the mountain he almost missed. *That's gotta be it,* thought Jr. *It's the last one.* Everyone was sure they'd found it. So, they all went into this one together. Like before, little Gio squatted down with ears erect, waiting to see what would happen. "Anything, Gio?" asked Owen.

"I'm sorry," he answered, tears streaming down his little cheeks. "I guess my ears aren't good enough or big enough or smart enough."

"Don't worry," Owen consoled him. "It's not your fault; it's our fault. We didn't bring you to the right caves."

Then Joaquin suggested, "Let's see if there are any caves are on the backside. Hop on my back, Jr."

"Wait!" exclaimed Owen. "A quick double-checking of these caves might be wise to ensure we didn't miss something. That way, we won't have to come back." So that's what they did, recheck each cave, starting with cave one.

By the time they got back to cave three, the one that gave Gio Jr. a strange feeling, the sun had shifted, so the light angle in the cave was a little further right than when he checked the first time. So, he entered and squatted down in the now sunny spot. When he closed his eyes to concentrate, his ears started vibrating like tuning forks so strongly it sounded like music. All the flyers could see something was happening.

"Now, Elsu," Grandpa said, pausing momentarily, looking only at me. "If you listen with your heart, mother nature will sing melodies to you even when no one else hears." Then he continued the story saying Gio Jr. was so excited he hopped up, but soon as he did, the tingling stopped.

"It's gone," he said. "I lost it. Dad will be so disappointed in me."

"No, he won't, no, he won't," squawked Morgan, "sit down again; again, sit down; you'll see."

"Go ahead," instructed Owen and Joaquin, crossing their feathers like fingers, "try it."

Again, Gio Jr. squatted, and though he felt like the whole cave was vibrating, he arched his little back and remained squatted this time. His ears started tingling again and the entire cave lit up so bright, momentarily it blinded everyone. As their eyes adjusted, the group was mesmerized by the cave walls made almost solidly of gold. And light was radiating around Jr.

"Move over, Jr. Let me see something," said Owen. "Morgan, can you scratch off that top layer of dirt?"

"Sure," replied Morgan. He began to scratch and claw, with dirt flying every which way while the others looked on anxiously. The deeper Morgan dug, the brighter the glow. Then tap, tap, tap, he hit something with the tip of his left claw. "I've hit something hard," said Morgan.

Owen leaned over to brush away the remaining dirt exposing a stone glowing like an ember. They were stunned by what they'd just found. "Is it hot?" asked Gio Jr.

Morgan leaned over and touched it with his foot. "Nope, cool to the touch." So, off they went, Gio Jr. on Joaquin's back, flanked by Owen and Morgan, with Owen gripping the precious rock in his strong claws. Morgan let out a piercing shrill to signal they were on their way.

"What a turn of events," chuckled Grandpa. "The magical artifact found miraculously, not by humans, but by forest creatures." This was way beyond the crew's wildest dreams or comprehension, as they soon would learn.

As a jubilant Sitka crew celebrated their good fortune, Captain John and his men combed the countryside by horseback to cover more ground, searching in vain for Coyoteville. Unfortunately, finding the lair of a pack of cunning, elusive coyotes was like trying to find a needle in a haystack. But anger knows no reason. So, in vain, they searched, governed by their wrath.

It was by sheer chance they did not hear the jubilation coming from nearby Coyoteville preceding the opening of the black box. Surely, they would have heard the shouts of surprise, followed by disbelief, when the coyotes discovered the coveted prize was not in the box, just a few souvenirs belonging to Captain John.

"We've been hoodwinked," yelled Kumar, the coup leader, "double-crossed by that lying half-breed Calvin. We must find him." But Calvin was long gone with at least a day's head start in a rugged, relatively unexplored region of dense forests, woods, hills, mountains, and caves, ideal hiding places. Again, it was the needle in the hay stack. However, Kumar was adamant about finding Calvin. So, in vain, he sent a small group of his best trackers to locate Calvin while John and his men, in vain, continued searching for them.

Meanwhile, no one was looking for the Sitka crew, who were basking in glory of finding the genuine artifact. But of course, being forest creatures, no one, not even Owen the oracle, could figure out how to tap its power. Well, no matter. It was now late afternoon, and lunch was way overdue. And nothing distracts forest creatures more than relaxing and munching on tasty treats. Not even magic.

While eating, Morgan amused them with some of his most infamous eavesdropping stories where the line between fact and fiction became blurry. Except, one particular story about Miner Mike caught their full attention.

Morgan described how one day he overheard Ovie the mule talking to Mike. He thought they would be shocked by this, a talking mule, but no one even blinked an eye as they knew this was true firsthand.

Morgan went on to explain that the long, dirty hair and unkempt attire, living in that dilapidated shack, was a sham. That Mike, in fact, was Indian, a member of the Miwok tribe that occupied the region long before John and his kind showed up. He told them Mike was a wise man in the tribe and understood the power of the nugget. And that it was a sacred relic of the Miwoks for generations.

"Are we talking about the same Miner Mike who came after me with a musket?" asked Gio in a snippy tone.

"Miner Mike knows, Miner Mike knows," squawked Morgan. Parrots, when excited, often say things twice.

"Well, I guess someone has to talk to Miner Mike, but it ain't gonna be me," shouted Gio gruffly.

"Do we have any volunteers?" asked Captain Will.

To Gio's surprise, Jenny spoke up, "I'll go, Captain. Perhaps he'll feel less threatened approached by a gentle female rabbit."

"Not without me," countered Gio, immediately taking a protective stance beside his wife.

Sunny skunk offered to join the mission, reasoning that if trouble broke out, he could disorient Mike with a dose of his powerful magic. "Good thinking," remarked Will.

"That's three volunteers, but we need four. We could use a flyer who can cause interference from above if needed." With that, Joaquin Hawk stepped forward.

Grandpa paused to explain why having a hawk on your adventure was good. "You know, hawks can see many times better than us. I've observed wild animals my whole life and have always been amazed by and felt a special kinship with hawks. They are powerful yet intelligent. They possess all the attributes of a perfectly designed hunter; sharp talons and a large curved beak ideal for capturing and tearing prey. With muscular legs, they can dive from the sky fast as a bolt of lightning. But they can also be gentle, quiet creatures. I know of no other animal that better captures the spirit and soul of our people. So yes, I would welcome a hawk like Joaquin by my side. That is why it was no surprise to me that Joaquin would step forward as the fourth member to engage Miner Mike and see if Morgan's story panned out."

Silent during this whole transaction was Gio Jr., who had no plans of his parents going on a dangerous mission without him. Instead, he was formulating his plan to tag along.

The rest of the evening, the crew led by Morgan conjured up wild stories about the rock's magical powers. "I'll bet the stone will grant three wishes if we rub it," smirked Akoni Raccoon.

"I'll bet it would make its owner invisible," added Sunny Skunk.

"Perhaps it will endow one with great strength of intellect to control the minds of others," stated Owen Owl.

"No, you're all wrong," said Gio, adding his two cents. "The stone would give me blinding speed so great I will run above the ground." Everyone laughed at that, including Gio.

"I'll bet it's just a rock, an ordinary rock like I see on the shoreline every day back at home," chimed in Sasha Beaver. "That's what it looks like to me." No one paid any attention to Sasha.

"Ok, everyone, let's call it a night," ordered Captain Will. "Big mission tomorrow."

After endlessly searching all day into the evening, Captain John and Kumar both gave up. They returned to their homes, still angry and swearing revenge on Calvin.

"What a beautiful morning," said Jenny Rabbit awakening the next day, trying to lighten the mood for the crew, knowing she'd be facing a challenging encounter with Miner Mike.

"Here, take this with you," Will said to Gio, handing him a small gunny sack filled with a few rocks.

"What's this for?" asked Gio.

"Just throw them at Miner Mike if things go bad. Hopefully, it'll distract him enough to escape before he grabs his musket."

"Thanks, Will, this will help me protect Jenny. She's my life, you know."

"I understand," gestured Will, his broad shoulders slumping. "Seems like I had someone like that once upon a time, but honestly, I can't remember. Well, good luck, Gio. May our ancestral spirts guide and protect all of you." And with that, they were off, with Joaquin scouting above for trouble.

Today would be a long, unsettling one for the rest of the crew. They had ventured before into the unknown together, ready for the unexpected. But this time, their comrades were marching straight into a known danger. An uneasiness consumed the Sitka this day. The crew kept themselves busy with chores as a distraction. Even the Sitka seems to be swaying gently in the current as if trying to ease their worry.

As the Sitka team maneuvered the terrain toward the river, Joaquin spotted none other than Captain John and his men heading back out for another futile search for Calvin. He signaled down to his comrades to take cover. Once this danger passed, they continued toward the river hoping to locate Miner Mike and Ovie.

Shortly, they arrived at Mike's cabin, where Jenny signaled for them to halt as she cautiously approached the porch. Since Ovie was not in the yard, she figured Mike was gone too, probably at the river panning for gold. They crossed the rickety wooden bridge and proceeded slowly up the river, trying not to surprise him. After a few miles, a hoarse-like screech by Joaquin signaled that something was ahead. First, they came across Ovie munching on some crabgrass, so they figured Mike couldn't be far off. They spotted him about 40 paces ahead, where the river bends, working his tin pan looking for gold. Amos noticed Mike's musket leaning against a nearby tree, so he hid it under some tall brush.

Ever so carefully, Jenny approached Miner Mike. Then, gently as possible, she introduced herself. "Good morning Mr. Mike. My name is Jenny, Jenny Rabbit. I believe you may have met my husband over there (pointing) when members of our crew accidentally trespassed on your property. Please accept our deepest apology. I assure you it won't happen again."

Mike just stood there, steely eyes fixed on Jenny, then glancing at Gio and back to Jenny. Amos moseyed around in the background, pretending not to be part of the goings-on. *At least he's not going for his musket*, thought Gio.

Everything was calm for the moment. Then, without warning, Gio Jr. popped out of the bag of rocks he had hid in and took a defensive position between the miner and Jenny with his little chest puffed out. "Don't you touch my mom," he threatened. Gio was rattled, trying to think quickly.

But Miner Mike just glanced down at the little rabbit and grinned. "How noble you are, little one, to risk yourself for your mother. I am Mike, but in my native Miwok tribe, they call me Notaku, which stands for growling bear." Then, Amos stepped forward, commenting to Notaku that their captain's name was Will, also known sometimes as growling bear. Everyone chuckled at that, and the tension lifted.

Well, it lifted for everyone except Gino, who was still peeved about Mike taking a shot at him with his musket. "I sense some uneasiness in you, Gino. If it's about that time I fired at you, know this, my friend. I never miss anything I intend to shoot."

Then, Notaku asked them to sit and share some acorn meal cakes, fish, and berries. "I know Captain John and his men make fun of Ovie and me. That's good they don't take us seriously. We Miwoks were here long before them working at peace with the land, taking only what we needed to nourish ourselves and survive. My ancestors arrived here during the great migration thousands of years ago tracking game across the great land bridge that appeared from nowhere."

"We gave thanks to this bountiful paradise and humbled ourselves for its abundant gifts; the wildlife to hunt, the fertile soil for planting, wild foods to gather all year, and the splendid trees and majestic boulders to shelter and protect us. And, of course, clean, pure water, the essence of life itself."

"We were blessed to live in harmony. Then came the marauders enslaving our people with their religion and diseases while plundering and pillaging this beautiful region. And for what? Gold! But not just any gold. A priceless artifact holding unspeakable mystical power protected by my ancestors for generations. In the wrong hands, it could be a devastating, destructive weapon. They sought to control its power for their selfish purpose. That's why every day, sun up to sun down, endlessly, I search, hoping to keep this powerful unnatural force secure from those who would use it for evil."

"Are you the only survivor of your tribe?" Jenny asked. "Where is your family?"

Notaku explained that John and others like him forced most of his tribe to toil in the crop fields, tend livestock, harvest timber, or perform other such labor. Over time their broken bodies and spirits shortened their lives, leaving but a handful to carry on. How Captain John learned of the magic stone, Notaku didn't know. But he did know he must prevent him from controlling its power.

"You understand its power?" asked Jenny. The rest of the Sitka team was all ears now.

Notaku explained what he'd learned from ancient stories passed down. "The stone triggers some form of gateway. This gateway can act as a portal transporting one to the future or past or just granting one sight into the future or past. It can be a gift or a curse. Its ominous power has destroyed many lives. No one knows its true origin or even the full extent of its power."

The team thanked Notaku for enlightening them and quickly left for the Sitka to brief the rest of the crew.

Harper and a few hands had just cooled down the horses and returned them to the stables while Captain John sat in the great hall seething and plotting over a shot glass of whiskey.

"And where is Calvin all this time, and what is he up too? And, more importantly, how much does he actually know about that rock he snatched? I wonder," said Grandpa. As I glanced around, I could see all the villagers trying to shift closer to Grandpa Liwanu, hoping to hear the answers to those questions.

Back at the Sitka, Captain Will (*the growling bear*, mused Grandpa) and the crew, having been thoroughly briefed by Jenny, had a lot to think over. The flyers and Sasha Beaver wanted to turn the stone over to Notaku. But Will, Jenny, and the others were captivated by the possibilities.

"Let's at least take it into the cave and see if it works," begged Jenny. "Maybe Mike is truly a crazy old miner, and that story he told us as Notaku was one he made up. But what if it's true?" Jenny desperately wanted to know who kidnapped her little son on their journey to New Helvetia. All mothers have long memories when it comes to their children, even rabbit moms. After talking it over, the crew unanimously agreed to test the stone, except for Sasha Beaver, who still maintained it was just an ordinary rock.

Grandpa paused and asked the children listening to the story, "What do you think? Is the stone magic or just an ordinary rock?"

I knew deep down the stone had to be real, but kept my thoughts to myself while I watched the other kids mumbling to each other with curiosity. I could tell even the parents weren't sure.

After letting that question fester for a bit, he tried to continue, but something was wrong. Grandpa stalled a little and seemed to lose his place. Father quickly grabbed him by his right arm and, with Mother's help, they took him to our hut. The villagers slowly gathered themselves and their children and headed home.

I bolted home to check on Grandpa. Father had laid him in his bed. I asked if I could see him, to which Father replied, "Yes, Elsu, but only for a moment. He is ailing." I did not know what ailing meant but figured it was not good.

"Grandpa, Grandpa, you okay?" I whispered.

"Yes, my hunter boy," he said, waving me to his side. "Grandpa is just tired. I'll be better tomorrow."

I told him that I loved him and shared my dream of being in the story he was telling.

"Dreams come true, Elsu," he murmured. "Dreams come true." Then he closed his eyes, and I went to bed.

Chapter 7
A Sad Beginning

The next day was the saddest of my life. Grandpa Liwanu would not meet me at the tree anymore for storytelling. He would not fish with me anymore or call me hunter boy. Though I had sensed this coming, it was still hard to believe he was gone. I would not see or hear him again or smell the sweet scent of lavender he always carried. Father's words did help soothe me. He always knew how to explain things according to our Miwok beliefs, which helped me understand times of joy and times of pain. And this was a most painful experience for me.

"I know how much you loved your grandfather and how much you'll miss him." I just shrugged my shoulders with my head down as Father continued, "We shall miss him too, Elsu. But we must not dwell on his passing but on his infinite spirit, for dying is a beginning, just like when you were born. We must treasure all these years with him and the gifts of wisdom and enduring love he gave us. He taught us to respect and honor our heritage, and there was no quit in him."

"I often think of my grandfather, Hanta, and that keeps him connected to me, not like just a fainting thought. I must not forget the life lessons he taught me and his voice, how he tilted his head when he spoke or leaned forward while laughing. Elsu, as long as you remember the wave," Father mimicked the motion with his hand, "you will always remember Grandpa."

That drew a smile from me, as I also mimicked Grandpa's signature motion. "Because you cannot see him means not that he cannot see you, Elsu. He exists now in a plane where the rivers bulge with fish, and game is plentiful. Where every arrow hits its mark, every battle is won, and the bear greets the deer." As Father spoke, it seemed like I could almost see Grandpa Liwanu and the mother bear with the fish, and I felt a little better, even hopeful.

"Now, Elsu, you must help me as we honor his life. I will announce his passing to the village this morning. There will be those who believe one passes into eternal nothingness; all they were is erased. Grandfather believed one passes into a higher plane than our earthly existence, and all things are possible in this plane. A place where dreams come true. Mother and I believe this too, and so must you, Elsu, so must you."

Then Father hugged me and told me to help Mother with the feast to honor Grandfather. As I walked over to where Mama and two of her closest friends were already busy with preparations, I couldn't help thinking about the unfinished story. It had become part of me and forever a link between Grandpa and me. Except now, I will never know how it all ends. That made me sad again.

With all the villagers who came to remember Grandpa Liwanu, I felt alone. Even Kono could not cheer me up. After the villagers laid him to rest near the river, I could not bear sleeping in my bed so close to his. So, I curled up between my parents.

The next few days were challenging as we tried to settle into a new normal without Grandpa. I longed for him to finish the story, and at night I dreamed I was a character in it. This particular night my sense of Grandpa near me was strong. So, I took a smidgeon of lavender from his pouch still hanging over his bed to help soothe me to sleep. As I lay on my bed half sleep and half-awake, I thought of the Sitka crew and wished with all my heart to join their adventure. I knew my dreams this night would be consumed by this one desire, one hope, one prayer.

***

The next morning, Enyeto was up early calling out, "Litonya! Litonya! Have you seen Elsu this morning? His bed is empty."

"Well, at least he's not mulling around here missing your father," she replied.

"Yes, but his bow is also missing. I hope he did not go hunting without me. He's still just ten years old. I'll look for him. If he went fishing, let's hope he catches a big one. Maybe he hiked upriver. I'll see if I can find him. He couldn't have gone far without the canoe." And then a thought hit me. *I wonder if he went to that last spot where he and Father caught that big salmon we roasted. I'll check there first.*

It was quite a hike without the canoe, but I found the spot, even the tree stump Father sat on. I decided to sit on it for a spell to rest and meditate. The stillness with faint sounds from the forest was soothing. As I sat there, "Enyeto," a voice called out. But when I turned to see, no one was there. For a second, I thought Elsu was playing a trick on me.

I yelled to him, "Come out, Elsu. Breakfast is ready. Time to eat." There was no reply. Again, I yelled, "Elsu, Mother will be unhappy that we delay eating the meal she's prepared." After several minutes with no response, I realized I was totally alone. So again, I closed my eyes to open my mind when I heard a chorus of voices calling "Enyeto, Enyeto," like echoes in the forest. "Know what we know, see what we see, feel what we feel," repeating over and over with vivid images of Father and Grandfather Hanta sketched in my mind.

At that moment, Father Liwanu's last words of the story came to me as a vision of what occurred next. I sprang up from the tree stump, yelling, *Of course, that's my calling now, to continue the story that began with Hanta, then passed to my father, Liwanu, and now to me.* Any thoughts I had about the story being a tale were gone now. I felt so much joy I hugged a tree and frolicked in my bare feet along the river's edge.

Then, with my hearting pounding and sweat pouring down my neck to my back and chest, I raced back to Litonya as fast as I could, thinking, *What if I'm not worthy and the visions desert me?* But deep down, I knew they would not.

"Litonya," I shouted, panting, "come outside."

Thinking something was wrong with Elsu; she ran toward me from the hut yelling with her arms raised in alarm. "Is he okay, Enyeto? Is my boy okay?"

With my shirt wringing wet, trying to catch my breath, I replied, "Yes, Litonya, he is fine, but I need you to fetch the villagers here right away. I have news for all to hear."

"He is not harmed? Then where is he? Tell me now!" She insisted on an answer, but with my forceful urging for her to fetch the villagers, finally, she obliged.

"Bring them to the story tree," I shouted, pointing in that direction as she left.

Once she returned with them, I sat down on the pine needles in Father's spot, trying to settle my nerves. I patted for her to sit next to me and the villagers to get comfortable. No one was allowed to sit in Elsu's spot between Litonya and me. I explained the episode that happened to me earlier and the revelation that I was next in line to pass on what happened to the Sitka and the crew. That Hanta and Liwanu were now channeling their story through me. As I picked up where Father left off, Litonya again asked, "Where is Elsu? Should we not wait for him, patting his spot on the pine needles?"

I replied, "Elsu will be here soon."

Then I began. Liwanu's last words were that Sasha Beaver claimed the magic stone was just a rock, but no one listened to Sasha. There was so much excitement aboard the Sitka that night it was hard to sleep. Everyone imagined out loud what they would do with mystical powers. Then Jenny made a key point. "We must take Notaku with us! He can help unlock the stone's magic."

"You're right, Jenny," replied Captain Will, "good thinking. Now, let's all get some shuteye."

Jenny added, "Yes, we want to take off in the morning long before the humans. I know they're up to something. They were out on horseback this morning."

"Sasha," commanded Will, "get some tea going before dawn to spark the crew."

"Sure thing, Captain."

At that moment, I believe the villagers realized the genuine story would continue through me. So, they shifted in closer to catch every word I spoke.

While the Sitka crew and Captain John's men were settling in for the night, Calvin emerged from his hiding place near the foothills. He was bent on finding the right cave to activate his stolen magic rock. Yes, he knew everything, compliments of one loudmouth parrot who can't keep his beak shut.

"If I can just locate the cave, everyone will bow down to me, and I will rule this kingdom. I will have my vengeance," his village's searing rebuke still burning like an open wound. A determined Calvin spent half the night relentlessly checking, rechecking, and triple-checking every cave in sight. None of them worked.

A little before daybreak, a demoralized Calvin slithered back to his hiding place to avoid discovery, unsure of his next move. Meanwhile, an eager Sitka crew, plus Notaku, returned to the same stretch of caves to begin the leg of their new adventure, the Magic Cave. Hearing voices nearby, Calvin skedaddled out of the cave he hid and slept in, not even knowing it was, in fact, the right cave. He just had the wrong rock.

"Now, which cave was it," remarked Amos Skunk.

Owen just smirked, "Leave it to me." Then, he signaled Joaquin to do a flyover with him. Joaquin spotted it immediately, a large S scratched into the soil on top of one of the caves. "I did that so we could locate it later," Owen boasted.

"Brilliant, absolutely brilliant, Owen," praised Joaquin.

The two flyers landed on the S and signaled with their wings to the others. Joaquin explained about the marker Owen had left. After some high-fives, Will asked, "Everyone ready? Owen, bring the stone. In we go."

Once inside, Gio Jr., anxious to impress his pop, instructed Owen where to place the stone to its original spot where he'd squatted. Once Owen did, light exploded like a prism inside the cave as the stone illuminated and the walls shimmered like cut glass. As their eyes adjusted, the shimmer faded to a golden hue. The whole episode felt otherworldly.

Notaku spoke first, "Now I know why I am here; to return to an earlier time, a time of peace and serenity among my people. I will prepare them for an uncertain future they could not envision. I need but desire this with all my being, and it will be so."

"I believe I understand now," said Captain Will.

Jenny asked if she might first try using the stone to resolve a nagging question. Will gestured affirmatively, so Jenny moved over close to the stone and raised her paws, eyes shut. Then, she concentrated with all her being on seeking the answer to who kidnapped her son.

A strange out-of-body experience consumed her as if suspended in midair. Afraid and curious, even with closed eyes, she could see her husband so clearly in the woods teaching little Gio to hide and him darting away too far. Then Gio, fraught with despair running back toward their camp as she felt herself reaching out to him. Finally, she witnessed the answer to her question, Warrick trotting away, holding her son in his mouth, only to be intercepted by Calvin and his family. Then the vision ended as abruptly as it began.

Jenny opened her eyes, tears tumbling down her pink bunny cheeks. Gio moved over to comfort her, but the vision was too troubling. "It was Warrick," she sobbed. "It was Warrick all along. And we trusted him. How could he betray us like that? How could he," she repeated, burying her face in her husband's chest for comfort.

After being in the cave for several minutes, their eyes fully adjusted to the brightness. They were able to see the walls covered almost entirely with gold. "We're rich, we're rich," shouted Akoni Raccoon, oblivious to the emotional distress Jenny and Gio were going through at that moment. Unfortunately, Akoni misunderstood the true wealth of the cave.

In life, we too often misunderstand what's truly valuable. I knew that wisdom came straight from my father still teaching us.

But Akoni was utterly irrational, mesmerized by the vast amount of glittering gold. He wasn't alone. Jonathan, Amos, Joaquin, and Morgan all began prying the gold from the cave walls even though they had no sacks to carry them. Never mind any mystical, magical mumbo-jumbo. Momentarily, their greed got the best of them.

Jenny, Gio, and Gio Jr. just wanted to return home to their cozy, comfortable cavern in the woods on Yerba

Buena Island. But, I am sure they would have great difficulty putting behind them what Warrick Wolf had done.

Captain Will yearned for something more than just visions. He confided in Notaku about his dreams of an earlier life. He recalled arriving on Yerba Buena from across the seas so long ago and his burning desire to understand who he was, where he came from, and why.

"Pardon Enyeto, but should we not wait for Elsu?" Litonya whispered, tapping on my shoulder. "He would not want to miss so much of the story."

"He will show up very soon, my wife. Trust me," as I continued. I sensed almost scornful compliance from Litonya for putting her off about the whereabouts of our son. Her intuition at this point was strong, her patience dwindling.

As Notaku was about to speak, who should show up at the cave entrance? None other than Warrick Wolf on his regular patrol of the mountainous region. Jenny Rabbit was furious, yelling, "You monster, you took my son; you took my son. We trusted you, fought side by side with you."

Before anyone could make a move, Warrick quickly responded, "I was returning your son, not kidnapping him."

"You better explain and fast," roared Gio, already moving toward Warrick.

Captain Will intervened, "Wait, hold on, let him finish." But even Will felt a twinge of anger thinking back to when Gio had been snatched.

Warrick sat down to put everyone at ease. Then with tears welling up in his eyes, he began explaining. "As you all know, I lost my family to the coyotes, my beautiful wife and my precious little sons. I still have nightmares of seeing their little blue eyes staring at me and blaming myself for not protecting them, my most sacred duty. When I saw your son, it all came rushing back to me. So, you see, I wasn't saving your son; I was saving mine."

"This was a chance to redeem myself I knew might never come again. While on patrol, I spotted you, pointing at Gio, practicing survival techniques with your son. I decided to sit and watch for a spell. Seeing the two of you together took me back to when I was training my sons. That was a special time in my life. I was reliving those moments watching how much little Gio looked up to you, longing for that part of my life I knew was gone forever."

"When you got separated, I was sure you would locate him, but then you left in a panic. I could see he was lost and frightened trying to find you, so I gathered him up and was on my way to your camp when Calvin and his clan showed up. I knew I was no match for that many varmints, so I gently lay him down and vamoosed. I've fretted about it ever since, thinking now I'd lost my sons and yours."

"That is, until I saw him at my cave with you two," pointing at Will and Jenny. "I was so relieved but knew at that very moment it was time to confront Calvin to make sure no one else's little one went missing. That's why I joined you in the crop fields, to finally redeem myself," a tear trickling down his face.

Believing Warrick's sincerity, the crew welcomed him into the cave. Warrick was stunned by the sheer brilliance, squinting his sharp wolf eyes, trying to focus. He'd heard the folklore of a magical cave but never really believed it. But here it was.

"Isn't that Miner Mike? What's he doing here?" drawing grins from everyone.

Miner Mike spoke, "My name is Notaku, and we are about to embark on a cosmic journey to forbidden times. Will you not join us? Myself, I will join my ancient Miwok family from long ago."

Will said he would enter the unknown to seek his true identity and purpose. Owen was noncommittal, so Warrick spoke, "I would give my life to reunite with my wife and sons. I'm unsure how this is possible, but I'm in."

On one side of the glowing cave stood Will, Notaku, and Warrick, ready to share one journey to three destinations. They locked arms and closed their eyes, hoping the magic nugget would grant their deepest wish. As the cave glowed even brighter they slowly began to fade away. At the last second, Owen grabbed Will's arm to make the journey too. Moments later, they were gone. "Maybe they're just invisible," commented Jonathan, waving the air his comrades just occupied only to fan empty space. There was nothing there. They were truly gone.

The rest of the crew sat there in disbelief. "Now what," asked Gio in a panic. "What do we do now?"

Jenny replied, "First, let's bury the stone. Second, we must solemnly pledge, swear on our very lives to keep this a secret," looking squarely at Morgan. "We must leave this cave as we found it for their return. Joaquin, make sure that 'S' on top of the cave is covered to hide it from others exploring the area. We must not leave any clues. Let's make preparations for our long journey home. None of what happens leaves this cave. Are we in accord?"

"Yes sir, I mean, Ma'am," said Gio with a salute. "That's my wife," he whispered proudly to Sasha Beaver.

Jenny could sense that the crew was struggling with losing their captain. She reassured them, saying, "Remember, Captain Will told us he would wear his bleached gold stitched Captain's hat to lead us on amazing quests across the seas. We all know he will keep his word. They will return." Ever so slowly, the cave began returning to normal.

Comforted by Jenny's words, the remaining crew gathered themselves, plus all the gold from the cave walls they could carry, and headed outside. Once there, they were surprised to come face to face with a young human boy at the mouth of the cave. Wondering if he had overheard them talking about the power of the cave, Jenny asked the youngster, "Who are you? Where did you come from?"

"I am Elsu," he replied. "I come from our village near the two great rivers." Then, with the alarm of a ten-year-old, he asked, "Where am I? Where are my mom and dad?"

As expected, Litonya sprang to her feet. "How is this possible? He cannot be my Elsu. It must be another boy named Elsu."

"Living near the two rivers, Litonya?" I said. "You know that all is possible in this story from the very fact that I am telling it to you through my ancestors. We must believe that everything in this story has a purpose and that Elsu would not be part of it if he had not willed it. All will unfold in time, Litonya. He will return to us, but only if the story continues."

Litonya repositioned herself in her spot next to me with renewed focus as I continued with our son speaking. "And you, you are (pointing) Jenny Rabbit, Amos Skunk, Akoni Raccoon, Sasha Beaver, Joaquin Hawk, Jonathan Fox, and that's Morgan Macaw over there." Morgan had shifted over to the lower branch of a nearby tree in eavesdropping position. "And that's your husband, Giovanni Rabbit, and son Gio Jr., right? My grandpa told me all about you guys!"

"Huh," the crew responded in disbelief.

"Where's Captain Will and Owen and Notaku?" asked Elsu.

"They're gone right now but hold on just a moment," said Jenny. "How do you know who we are?"

"I know your whole story since your crew left Yerba Buena Island aboard the Sitka," replied Elsu. "My great-grandpa Hanta had a special connection with your Will the bear, ever since he saved him from trappers and raised him from an orphan cub. Will granted Hanta the ability to know what he knew, see what he saw, and feel what he felt. Since Hanta's death, this connection passed to my grandpa Liwanu who has been telling me your story till now. Since I'm his grandson, maybe he will continue the story with my father through me since Will the bear is gone."

"But I don't belong here. I just wished, hoped with all my might, to see all of you, and somehow, here I am. Please, can you send me back home? I belong with my family. My mom will be worried."

"Shhh, calm down, little one," said Jenny in a soft, soothing voice as she gently hugged Elsu. "If you've been following our story through your grandpa, then you know all the wondrous things that happened to us. So, you must also know that with the powerful magic we possess, we can return you home this very moment if that is your wish."

"My wish! My wish was to join your journey, as I told Grandpa Liwanu, and here I am." Elsu thought for a moment. "If it's okay with you, I will join your crew for now. I think that is what he would want me to do."

"Then welcome aboard, Elsu. You are now a member of the Sitka crew. Meanwhile, you can still connect to your grandpa and him to you. And now, he'll be telling the story of your adventure too."

Slowly lifting his head upward, then lowering it, Elsu replied with a tear in his eye, "That cannot happen now. Grandpa passed a few days ago."

"I am so sorry, Child," Jenny whispered, embracing him as only a mother could. "Well, you have a new family for the time being, and we all look out for each other," her paw pointed at the crew. "Ok, Elsu?"

"Ok," Elsu answered.

"Now, Elsu, I want you to meet my son, Gio Jr.," as she waved him over. "He's much younger than you and could use a big brother to teach him stuff." Elsu glanced at Gio Jr., who gave him a thumbs up. "Can you help him out till you get back home?"

"Oh sure," said Elsu.

So, while Elsu didn't have his immediate family with him, at least for the time being, he had a little brother. However, this little brother was an extraordinary rabbit from a litter of one who had long yearned for a sibling. Plus, now he was part of the Sitka adventure. He was about to grow up fast, and I think he sensed that.

The Sitka crew, minus two crew members with a newcomer Miwok Indian boy, continued their journey. They maneuvered down the mountainside through the woods toward the Sitka to plot a course for home. Unbeknownst to them, Calvin coyote had witnessed the whole goings-on. Once they left, he entered the cave just in the nick of time, also transporting to whereabouts unknown as the magic from the rock faded away.

Exiting the woods to a clearing a short distance from the Sitka and Captain John's compound, they spotted some of John's men lurking around their vessel. One stood aft deck, and another was near the bow as if on guard duty. *Now, what are they up to?* she wondered.

Chapter 8
Who's Fooling Who

"Hold on, everyone. Let's watch this for a minute till we figure out what's happening."

A short time later, the two men got off the Sitka and were replaced by two more. Jenny recognized one of them as Harper from the dinner they attended at Captain John's place. She was stunned. "They're not guarding the Sitka. Captain John has seized it."

"What do we do now?" cried Sasha Beaver, banging his powerful tail angrily on the ground. "We can't get home without our boat. And I'm sure not swimming all the way back home."

They retreated to the woods, hiding amid a cluster of tall pines to consider their predicament. Johnathan Fox mumbled, *I hope they don't find the gold.*

I'm sure Gio Rabbit was thinking, *I hope they don't find the carrots.*

"Everyone shush," whispered Jenny, "this is serious. We have to think of something." Elsu and Gio Jr. were busy playing hide and seek.

Then an idea came to Jenny. "I need two crew members to sneak close to the Sitka. Let's see, Morgan, can you find a tree perch close enough to eavesdrop on those two?"

"My pleasure," replied Morgan.

"And Sasha, can you get near the boat underwater and do the same?"

"Sure," said Sasha.

"Great. Just get close enough to listen. Maybe we can find out what Captain John is up to. But, be very careful," counseled Jenny with a look of concern.

Off Morgan flew, circling the river's backside. He found a oak tree offshore just close enough to the Sitka to ease drop. Sasha slipped down the shore about fifty yards. Then, he doubled back underwater near the Sitka's stern. The rest of the crew nervously waited while Elsu and Gio Jr. were discovering the joys of having a brother. Litonya and I snuck a sly glance at each other as I continued.

Harper sat by the Sitka's tiller, grumbling, *Why must I babysit this bloody contraption. I'm no average bloke. Remove the rudder, says I. Boat can't maneuver absent a rudder, says I. But all I get is a bollocking from Captain Wobbly. I've had bugger to do all morning 'cept this doggy exercise. A damp squid, all it is, I tell you, a damp squid.*

At that point, Harper shouted to his partner sitting atop the front portion of the cabin, "How goes it, mate?"

Jake responded, "Bored out of me bloomin mind," mocking Harper and eliciting a chuckle from him. "How you doin?"

To which Harper replied, "Peachy. All is hunky dory, just hunky dory. Jake, how long you think we have to guard this old crate?"

"Well, Captain says he has to get that gold from Will soon's they return, mean' in their boat is commandeered as such."

"You mean we have to stay here till the animal crew gets back?"

"Righto," said Jake to which Harper complained, "A pile of rubbish says I. A heapin pile of rubbish!"

By this time, Morgan had shifted a few branches to get even closer to the Sitka until Jim spotted him while leaning back to stretch. Immediately, Morgan pretended to be asleep. "Hey Liverpool (Harper's sometimes nickname). Check out big beak up there. Wonder if it talks. Better not be eavesdropping on us."

Eyes closed, Morgan kept silent and still. Then Harper yelled, "Hey, you feathery wanker, be gone, I say." He gulped down the rest of a pint he'd been nursing and threw the mug at Morgan, startling him off his perch. Morgan flapped his wings with a screeching aark.

As he bolted from the tree, he yelled at Jake, the closest to him, "Si long ventouses (so long, suckers)," before crashing into the very next branch.

"Wanker bird, can't speak English, can't fly straight either. No worry there." Jake nodded in agreement. Morgan flying into the tree branch brought a hearty laugh from Harper and Jake, causing them to dismiss him as any kind of threat.

Having picked up this vital tidbit about the gold, Sasha and Morgan made a beeline for the forest to brief Jenny on what they'd heard. Morgan was a bit late, having banged into that branch beak first. He was trying to beat Sasha back to be the first to share the news. But he forgot that Sasha had to swim back downriver to go ashore, then double back to the forest. So bruised beak Morgan still arrived first, explaining, "They're after your gold, after your gold they are, yep, yep, after it," he reported.

"Mmm, so it's gold John's after," surmised Jenny. "He has no idea about the cave gold. So, we can use that to our advantage. We can offer him the lion's share of the tree stump gold in exchange for a business agreement. It was on his land anyway, so I'll use that angle."

Gio, who'd been quiet till now near the stern area listening to his wife reason through options, looked toward the other crew beaming. "See how smart she is. That's my wife, you know," as if they hadn't heard that about a million times.

Despite having to focus on the tasks at hand, Jenny couldn't help thinking about Notaku, Warrick, Will, and Owen and where their extradimensional journeys took them. But, then, something dawned on her, *What about Ovie mule? Who'll take care of him? Need to call a meeting right now to figure that out and plan our next move.*

Jenny called the crew over and began explaining her thoughts and ideas. "As Morgan and Sasha reported, now we know Captain John is after the gold Will discovered at the tree stump. Since he doesn't know about the cave gold, I propose we offer him two-thirds of the gold we stashed on the Sitka. We can trade that gold for a signed agreement letting us harvest on his land, except for gold. This contract will provide us with all the produce we need, plus we have a secret source to mine all the gold we want far away from John's property. And let's not forget the Sitka's tipping problem. We must be careful not to weigh her down with too much gold.”

Jenny stunned the crew with the ingenuity of her plan. “I guess she really is brilliant,” Johnathan Fox murmured to Joaquin.

“I’m confident this will work,” offered Jenny. “Are we together on this?”

The crew erupted with, “Hip-Hip Hooray for Captain Jenny.”

For once, Gio stayed silent and just smiled. But Gio Jr. yelled, “That’s my mom.”

Then Elsu added, “She sounds like my mom too.” A bond was developing quickly between Elsu and his new animal family.

“Now that’s settled,” said Jenny, “there’s one more little problem. With Notaku gone, there’s no one to care for Ovie. Any suggestions?”

“Well, Captain John has been one way or another in taking care of Notaku and Ovie on his land,” mentioned Joaquin. “And he does seem to have a soft spot for dogs; maybe he’ll take in Ovie once he discovers Notaku is gone. I suggest we go find Ovie and convince him to just wander onto John’s compound.”

“Ark, ark,” squawked Morgan. “Since I’ll be gone with you guys, he can be the new eavesdropper. Who’d suspect a talking mule, I say, talking mule!”

“That’s a fantastic idea, Morgan. We can’t trust humans much, so having Ovie as our boots on the ground may pay big dividends. Can you give him some eavesdropping tips?” asked Jenny.

“Of course, of course,” replied Morgan.

"Okay. Akoni, take Morgan to talk with Ovie tomorrow while Gio and I meet with Captain John."

"What time do you plan to meet with him?" asked Joaquin.

"I suggest earlier in the day before he drinks a pint or something else. Sometimes, humans get agitated and even dangerous when drinking, especially toward animals. I'll keep guard nearby if you need me."

"Good thinking," replied Jenny. "I'll take Gio with me since he seems to be so fond of him. The sun's going down, so take Sasha and Amos to scavenge for food. Elsu will need something to eat and help him sleep. He's had a long day, and tonight he'll miss his human family terribly. I'll review and re-review our plan for tomorrow with Gio," lowering her brow, casting a worrisome look his way.

"Aye, aye, Captain," Joaquin saluted. Jenny was starting to get used to this new role of captain.

Huddled around a much smaller than usual Sasha Beaver campfire to lay low, the crew and Elsu retired for some much-needed shuteye. Joaquin and Morgan stood guard high in a redwood. The rabbit family snuggled around Elsu like a warm blanket, and he felt secure. While sleeping, Elsu dreamed of his human family, especially Grandpa wishing he were there to share in his journey and adventures.

Tension hugged the morning as the crew would be facing a defining day. Captain Jenny and Gio again prepared for their meeting with Captain John. Then, off they went to his compound home. Stopping short of his front door by two rifle-toting goons, Jenny stated, "We represent the Sitka group. Captain John will be expecting us."

"Just hold on right there," said the two men, pointing their weapons up and noses down at the two critters in front of them. One stayed put while the other entered John's residence to check out Jenny's claim.

Immediately, Captain John emerged, greeting them to join him for refreshments. Once inside, Jenny got right to the point. "We're missing a couple of our crew, Captain Will and Owen Owl, so I've assumed captain's duties for now."

"Sorry to hear that. Hope they're okay." replied Captain John.

"Thank you," Jenny said as she continued, "In his absence, Captain Will instructed us to return to Yerba Buena Island and said he would find a way back home. However, it appears you have seized our vessel."

Captain John, rising from his chair, quickly denied this charge. "Listen here. We're just guarding the Sitka against transient looters looking for an easy mark as a favor to Will." Then, he reminded Jenny, "You know, Captain Will agreed to share any proceeds in exchange for harvesting on my lands. And in return, I assured him no interference from any humans. I've kept my end of the bargain. Except now, I'm actually guarding his boat. That was not part of the deal. No one has gotten with six feet of your precious Sitka. Just the other day, my men ran off some snoopers, trying to sneak onboard."

John rattled on till Jenny cut him off, saying, "I am well aware of that accord, and I am here to address that with you, Mr. John."

"Oh, stop with the formalities. Just call me John."

"Ok, John. On behalf of Captain Will, I propose we formalize an agreement in writing that we can use as visible proof to other humans. That way, we can protect both our shares of any proceeds."

"Yes, yes," stammered John. "That's all well and good. I'll have the paperwork drawn right away."

From left field came a totally loopy comment from Gio, "Excuse me, John, but I haven't seen any carrots growing in your pastures."

"I'll grow all the carrots you can eat, Gio," almost yelling as he paced back and forth, his brow rippled with frustration. "Can we just get on with it?" glaring at Jenny. Finally, she tabled what John had been angling to discuss the whole time—gold.

"Right now, our proceeds include crops harvested from your field, odds and ends from a sunken wreckage downriver, and gold we discovered upriver near Miner Mike's cabin. I'm certain you're interested in the gold?"

"Who wouldn't be," replied John, giving Jenny his full attention.

Before Gio could blurt out something else, Jenny offered, "Since we found the gold on your land, I propose you take two-thirds share, double ours."

"Done, done," said John, cutting Jenny off while pouring himself a stiff shot of brandy. Then he told her, "This is a good deal, a good deal for us both." But really, he was thinking to himself, *Animals will never be as smart as humans. This is a raw deal for her.*

I can say, at this point, John didn't trust any of the animals and wasn't sure which of them had the stone he so coveted. His suspicions clouded his clear thinking about the animals being forthright and honest.

"It's settled then," stated Captain Jenny. "You will remove your men from the Sitka and draw up the agreement. We will sign it tomorrow and turn over your share of the gold." A hand-to-paw handshake sealed the deal. But once they touched, a cold sensation quivered through Jenny, raising the hair on her back and causing her to jerk her paw away. Of course, John dismissed this as just a reaction from a mindless animal.

Jenny and Gio left, running full speed across the field to fetch the crew back to their beloved boat. Midway, they paused for Jenny to catch her breath. "Wasn't quite sure how that was gonna go, Gio. But (they uttered together), you can always count on greedy humans," chuckling as they scurried the rest of the way back to the woods.

As they arrived, Gio shot ahead of Jenny so he could boast. "She was fantastic; had old John eating out of her hand. Now we can go home."

"And get Elsu home when he's ready," added Jenny, fondly glancing Elsu's way.

I saw the relief on Litonya's face as I described how the crew collected themselves and headed for the Sitka in the blazing afternoon heat. "Whew," griped Jonathan Fox, "never this hot on Yerba Buena!"

"I'm headed straight for the water," said Sasha Beaver.

"Me too," added Elsu.

"Me three," Gio Jr. chimed in, drawing a puzzled look from Gio and Jenny and laughter from the rest.

"A swimming rabbit, that'll be the day," Sasha smirked. "The day he swims, I'll climb a tree." More laughter erupted from the group except for Gio Jr. and Elsu, who just looked on curiously.

"Well, I know our son can swim, Litonya, but a rabbit?"

"As you said earlier, Enyeto, anything is possible in this story. But I need to say it is dinner time. Shall we meet tomorrow after chores to continue?"

Everyone nodded, so Litonya and I headed for our hut. "It's been quite a day, my wife, hasn't it?"

"Yes, Enyeto," she responded, "it's been quite a day."

As we sat at our table for supper, seeing Elsu's seat empty and not eating with him was strange, but I knew he would be around tomorrow. As usual, Litonya set a place for him at the table. She also placed some lavender in the bowl where my father usually sat in remembrance. That touched my heart. Closing my eyes for a moment, I could see one of his dismissive waves aimed my way, and I smiled. Life is so uncertain as each day promises a new beginning. Watching my beautiful Litonya maneuver around our hut preparing dinner, I thought, *How precious and fragile life is*. Then I thought of Father now with his beloved Papina. A flow of emotions washed over me as I realized Litonya and I would share our forever too.

We awoke to a morning showering us with sunshine and warmth—an omen signifying joyful spirits. Litonya left for the village to toil the acorns, but to her surprise, the village women had already finished. With their husbands and children, they arrived anxious to hear more of the story. "The village came early today eager for the story, Husband. Perhaps my acorn days are finished," she mused.

Though I had not yet completed my morning chores, I had to admit that I, too, was eager to see what happened next with our son now in the story. So, I picked up right where I had left off the day before.

Across the grassy meadow, the crew strode till they reached their precious Sitka. She'd always been there for them, their anchor steady and true. She was truly their home away from home. Just being near her seemed to connect them to Yerba Buena Island, beloved family, and friends, and they all could feel that.

Captain John's men had already vacated, so they boarded their vessel and conducted a thorough inspection bow to stern, as ordered by Captain Jenny. They checked the freshness of the stored crops and whether the gold was still securely hidden in the bilge area. Because, no gold, no deal. All felt normal except for the absence of Will and Owen.

Munching on some leftover berries and nuts picked the previous evening, the crew lounged on the deck while Gio Jr. was getting a swim lesson from big brother Elsu. "Once you're in the water, move your arms and legs like this to float." Then he mimicked the action with his arms and legs.

"Huh," said Jr.

"Oh, sorry, I mean, move your front and back paws; like this. See?" Elsu again tried to demonstrate.

"Oh, this otta be good," Sasha whispered to Jonathan, leaning back against the cabin wall, ready to heckle.

Jr. hit the water with speed and agility like he'd been swimming his entire existence. He flipped on his back as he surfaced, gliding with a perfect backstroke. "He's not a rabbit," claimed Sasha. "He's some kind of waterfowl, a duck or fish or something."

Jonathan countered, "No, he's truly a special litter of one."

The water frolicking continued for at least another hour as Jenny gazed down lovingly at them from near the rudder. "They'll sleep well tonight. In the morning, I'll ask John for Harper's help checking for mechanical problems."

"Sounds good to me, Capitan," said Gio.

"Ok, stop that," directed Jenny. "We need to be a team, you and I (Jenny pointing at him) from now on, together. I can't do this without you."

Gio's eyes swelled up with tears realizing his precious, adoring wife needed him. A loving embrace topped it off for Gio.

Back at the river, Elsu was thinking, *I've never seen a rabbit swim like that. He swims better than I do, and my father taught me. He swam and caught fish in the river with his bare hands.* (Reminiscing) *I wish Grandpa Liwanu were here to see this. I miss him so much. I hope he's seeing what I see, feeling what I feel*, lowering his head, a little disheartened.

Back on the Sitka by the cabin, Akoni was looking for a tall tree for Sasha to shimmy up while Sasha was trying to understand how a rabbit could swim better than him. "Well, there's just one logical explanation," offered Akoni. "He's a better beaver than you are," laughing so hard he had to hold in his stomach.

All the villagers laughed along too.

Sasha was not at all amused. "Tell you what I think, Akoni. I think it's because of this expedition we're on."

"Explain," challenged Akoni raising both arms in obvious disagreement.

"Well, look at him," continued Sasha. "He's longer and leaner than his parents with less fur. Typically, rabbits spend their whole lives burrowed in one meadow, forest or wetland, eating weeds, grasses, wildflowers, and vegetable plants. During the winter, they munch on twigs, bark, buds, and anything green they can find. Remember, Gio was born on the Sitka. He's been on the move ever since, eating all sorts of different food with us, stuff rabbits don't normally eat cause they're too hard or dangerous to find. He hasn't spent his days in some rabbit warren hiding from predators. He's been on the move his entire short existence. That's why he's a lean, mean swimming machine."

"And the main reason," boasted Sasha. "He's been watching my superb swimming skills this whole trip," mimicking swimming moves with his arms and paddle tail.

"Oh yeah," smirked Akoni, rolling his eyes. "That explains it."

"Hey, you wisecracking me?" challenged Sasha.

"Oh no," replied Akoni. "I think you're really on to something. Maybe you should schedule a swimming lesson for the whole crew," as he strode toward the bow to ask Jenny if he had dinner duties. Sasha dove into the river for a quick swim to cool off.

With lots of leftover grub from John's crop fields, Jenny summoned everyone to dinner. Later, the remaining seven of the Sitka crew, eight counting Gio Jr. along with Elsu and Morgan relaxed on the deck, bellies stuffed full. Then, as dusk consumed evening, stars promenaded across the vast darkness. "Too bad Owen's not here," remarked Amos.

"Yes, and Will," threw in Akoni. "At least, they're together wherever they are."

"And let's not forget Notaku and Warrick," said Amos. "I wonder what their adventures are. I sure hope Warrick finds peace."

After taking a short break to refuel with an acorn cake topped with some tasty wild berries, I explained to the villagers that Warrick found that and much more in his brief trip back in time. Standing on a boulder crowning a high mountainous ridge looking strong and youthful, he gazed down on a magnificent valley below that looked familiar and then again not. As Warrick surveyed with keen wolf eyes, momentarily he locked stares with some creature far off in the distance, partially hidden by tangled overgrown brush. Warrick froze for a second, and it was gone. A flood of thoughts and emotions coursed through him as he dared to think, *Was that her*?

Kono's father waved at me to ask, "How do you know where Warrick went?"

I explained that this gift's channeling power enabled me to know what they know, see what they see, and feel what they feel. Will the Bear's gift was a gateway to all those in the story and what they knew, saw, and felt. That was how I knew Will and Owen's longer cosmic journey landed them in a strange land in the future where a time warp continuum transformed their state of being. Hopefully, Will gained clarity about his memories there.

I reminded the villagers about Notaku's claim that no one knew the full power of the stone. So, we should expect anything in this story. I could tell this added to their level of interest.

As they looked at me inquisitively, I explained that Notaku's journey back in time was no less epoch.

Appearing from nowhere among an entire civilization (as it was) of Miwoks, Notaku mistook this for heaven. He saw babies carried in homemade baskets, earthen ovens heated by hot stones, and natives dressed in colorful animal skins dancing around tattooed from head to toe wearing spectacular headdresses.

This journey for Notaku had seemed long but was just a blink of an eye, a irreconcilable experience, he just accepted as his destiny. And the purpose of that destiny was clear to him; to find words to prepare his heritage, a prideful, fearless, trusting nation for a future they could not conceive. Also, to understand the origin of the magic that brought him there.

Lastly, there's the burning question. Where did Calvin coyote go, and why? I could see the curiosity mounting among the villagers, especially the children.

Yes, many questions plagued the Sitka crew about these things. But for now, the present commanded their full attention and ours as well.

"Enyeto, I hope and pray that when these Sitka crew do get home, my Elsu will know he must come home too. As his father, I am certain you miss teaching him to hunt and fish in the woods and rivers. What greater companionship exists than life's episodes with father and son. The father teaches life lessons, and the son gains knowledge and wisdom."

"For a father, adoration from his son is the nectar of life itself. For me, Enyeto, his growth into manhood is both painful and fulfilling. I must release him as a child and embrace him as a man; while Child in my heart, he will always remain. Now, I wish that Child home with me for youth is fleeting, and I am selfish for that as any mother would be."

"I share your unease and discomfort, Litonya. And yes, your assessment strikes a nerve deep inside me. I, too, fret for his safety yet thrill in the Sitka's adventures that he now shares. I am sure he feels our yearning for his return." I held Litonya's hand, hoping our son could feel what we felt at that moment before I resumed the story.

Jenny followed up with Joaquin, "You located Ovie and got him squared away, right?"

"Oh yes, Captain, I almost forgot. Morgan fully briefed Ovie, and he liked the idea of being an undercover crew member. It seemed to give him a new purpose replacing caring for Miner Mike."

"Good, very good," Jenny thanked Joaquin.

They rejoined the crew on the deck fabricating stargazing stories absent Owen the regaler. "Hey, look at that one," said Amos, pointing. "Doesn't it look like an owl wearing glasses?"

"Yeah, yeah," answered Sasha. "And shhh, it looks like it's about to speak." First quiet, then robustious laughter erupted.

"What are they talking about?" our son asked.

Gio took Elsu aside to explain. Luckily, Gio had a great answer for him. "Well, let me see, Elsu," then waiting a few minutes to build suspense. Finally, Gio explained, "Orion the hunter is your star, one of the brightest up there."

"Really?" reacted a wide-eyed surprised Elsu. "So, I am the hunter?" mimicking the motions of slaying some animal with a bow and arrow. "Just like my father and grandpa?"

His spirits were greatly lifted by this revelation, and so were mine.

They returned to the deck with Elsu much more attentive to the stargazing session. Miraculously, this little chat with Gio gave him a much-needed identity as the newest crew member. No one understood needing an identity more than Gio. Unfortunately, he failed to fully understand the significance of his gift to our boy, but we did.

One by one, each animal identified a star they claimed looked like them, along with a fantastic yarn. It must have felt good to cut loose and have some fun knowing that they would cast off for home in the morning.

And morning came none too soon.

They were all up at the crack of dawn. So was Captain John pacing back and forth on the dock where the Sitka was tied, waiting for his gold.

Captain Jenny and John traded morning pleasantries, then got right down to business. "I'll have my crew unload all the bags of gold to the dock. Then, one of your men can double-check the Sitka cargo spaces to verify they're all accounted for," offered Jenny. "Then, we can sign the agreement, and you can take your two-thirds share. While doing that, would you mind if Harper checked our vessel for mechanical problems? Don't want any snafus on our trip home."

"Fine by me," replied John. "I've got the agreement right here. But, before we sign, do you mind if I check each gold bag first?"

"Sure, go right ahead," said Jenny. Though she was curious why John needed to check all the bags, she shrugged it off as no consequence.

She hopped down to the dock to witness John's meticulous, touchy/feely inspection of each bag, after which he separated his share. Then, they executed the agreement with a hand-to-paw handshake stomached by Jenny.

Harper reported that all looked sound mechanically. However, he told them they would need to replenish their fuel supply in a few days. "You may desire to have one of your waterfowl check the hull. Bottoms up to you," Harper said as he left their boat.

Once John and his men departed with their gold, Jenny ordered Amos and Akoni to fire up the engine as a quick test and then shut her down. "Sasha, once they finish, I want you to conduct a thorough check of the hull," ordered Jenny.

"The what?" Sasha asked, looking puzzled.

"The bottom of the boat," explained Jenny.

"Oh! Righto, Captain."

"Did you know what a hull was?" Litonya kidded me.

"My canoe has a bottom, not a hull," I quipped, drawing one of those smirks only a wife can make as I continued. A little while later, Amos, Akoni, and Sasha reported the engine steady and the hull intact.

Chapter 9
Homeward Bound

At long last, they were ready to head home. The crew took a solemn moment to reflect on all that'd happened and think about the long journey ahead. Theirs was an adventure for the ages, and to tell the truth, not yet over. Surprisingly, a somberness about leaving washed over them. Many experiences, good and bad, had become part of their being. New Helvetia would forever be a part of them now. Secretly, a few of the crew even fantasized about returning. Jenny knew deep down that a return trip was inevitable and not just for business reasons.

Scanning the area one last time, she spotted Ovie the mule flanked by Lance and Terrance bent over, munching on some tasty wild grasses. "That gold was well spent," she thought to herself.

John figured he got the best of the deal from the clueless animals since he swindled them out of the lion's share of the gold and confirmed, just to be sure, that they didn't have the odd-shaped magical nugget.

"What would you choose, the gold or the magic nugget?" I asked the children listening.

Nearly all the them and most of the adults shouted, "The nugget, we would take the magic nugget." They fantasized about what they would do with it for several minutes, so I waited a bit before picking up the story.

I wondered what our ancestors would have thought of that answer as I repeated Jenny's orders, "Grab those oars; let's take her out." Slowly but surely, the big paddlewheels began to turn as the Sitka cleared the dock. "Start the engine, Akoni," the resilient new captain shouted over the welcome sound of water lapping against the hull. And just like that, they cruised up the river with the current at about three knots. As the humans and New Helvetia faded away, the Sitka thrust toward home with every turn of its paddlewheels.

"We'll travel daily till afternoon, then find a place to dock overnight just as we did coming."

"Aye, Captain," the crew responded.

As they settled in for the trip, Morgan called Jenny aside to speak privately. "Ms. Jenny, my family, the McCaws, live at the lagoon. I must fly over to check on them and explain I'll be away on a trip, ark, on a trip for a while. I'll catch up to the Sitka downriver the next day or two. Can you tell the crew, so they don't panic when I land on the tea kettle? And please, tell Sasha not to make tea?"

"No worries. Our best to your family," Jenny replied. One big salute, and Morgan was off.

Jenny rejoined the crew, passed along Morgan's message, and finally took time to relax with her extended family. The Sitka cruised comfortably at about five knots on tame currents with temperatures cooling the farther downriver they traveled.

Having to coordinate with Captain John and make preparations aboard the Sitka made for a shortened day. So, before long, it was time to dock. As Joaquin flew in loopy circles searching for the right spot, an animated Gio hopped up and down, pointing, "over there, over there to the right," trying mightily to impress his wife. As it turned out it was a perfect spot with a wide angle to navigate into and away from any prying eyes. There was even a large, sturdy tree limb to tie the Sitka to.

"Gio, take Amos and Akoni. Canvass the area but don't venture too far and report back. We'll make camp here on the riverbank." Gio was touched Jenny would trust him with this major task.

This exchange between Gio and Jenny made me think about my beautiful Litonya and how much she trusts and supports me. I felt just like Gio at that moment.

"Won't let you down, Captain," Gio mused.

Jenny just chuckled and let that one slide. "C'mon, Elsu and Jr., help me unload some grub while Sasha makes one of his special campfires, glancing his way. And Sasha, be sure to save any extra timber for fuel."

"Too bad they did not take our son with them," I added. "He's only ten years old, but he knows his way around the outdoors hunting with Father and me." Litonya nodded in agreement.

Inspired by his wife, Gio took charge, fanning his team out about a hundred yards in different directions to scout the area. Finally, after half an hour of finding nothing to report, they returned to camp.

Akoni ran into Amos first and proposed a little joke to play on Gio, plus a wager. "Amos, I bet you five gold pieces; if I throw a rock at Gio, he'll bolt faster than lightning." Akoni was already laughing as he spoke.

"You're on," replied Amos.

They snuck around till they spotted Gio near some high brush relieving himself. "Oh, this is too perfect," chuckled Akoni. He grabbed a large rock, reeled his arm back, and threw it, bouncing off a tree and landing a few feet from where Gio was crouching. But Gio didn't even flinch, fully intent on executing his team leader role assigned by Jenny. So, instead of bolting, he swiftly whirled around, teeth bared in attack mode to face whatever threat there was.

"Bet you didn't expect that," snickered Amos. "And speaking of bets, you owe me five gold pieces. You can pay me once we reach home."

Akoni was stunned and visibly embarrassed at his wager. "Okay, but let's just keep this our little secret."

"Right, that'll cost you an extra gold piece," said Amos.

"Alright. Just remember, mom's the word."

With a thumbs up from Amos, they moved toward Gio, calling his name to avoid startling the ferocious bunny. Then, the three returned to the Sitka just in time for dinner.

By this time, Morgan was enjoying a joyous reunion with his family, mom and pop McCaw, little sister Tiki and brothers Charlie and Lago (short for Lagoon). There was a whole lot of arking going on. Morgan filled them in on his recent adventures. He explained that he was there for a short overnighter, then off on the steamboat Sitka to seek his fame and fortune. Of course, that led to a question from Tiki, "What's a steamboat?"

The McCaw family migrated from St. Lucia long ago to this lagoon that resembled home and had everything they needed to survive. The thick, abundant tree clusters filtering the sunlight and wind created a virtual rainforest environment. This exquisite microclimate produced lush vegetation yielding plentiful amounts of nuts, berries, and seeds to munch. Towering bluffs with a waterfall spanning several degrees temperature between the top and the exquisite lake it serviced was the crowning feature of this unique location.

"The only problem was not enough humans to eavesdrop on, a specialty of Morgan but a family pastime as well. You see McCaws need lots of mental stimulation and can be easily bored, leading to health issues. So, Morgan being a master at eavesdropping, was the healthiest McCaw in the entire lagoon taking great risks to sharpen his craft. So, he figured this adventure aboard the Sitka would be an eavesdropping bonanza."

I could tell from Litonya's expression that it was time to change from story time to dinnertime. The villagers gathered themselves and waved goodbye saying, "We'll be back tomorrow with lunch and dinner for you both."

Seems they are expecting a full day of the story, I thought.

I must say, I felt a sense of relief I could continue Hanta and Liwanu's story so that the villagers wanted to hear it, especially since Father brought his own style to tell it. *You can't replace a father or grandfather,* I thought. I really missed my papa. I missed my mother too, but I was much younger when she passed. Father always had a way of keeping her memory alive for me. I loved him for that. Now that he was gone, my sole link to my mother Papina was gone too, a tie that can never be again.

Losing Father felt like losing them both. Though he taught me that upon passing, our spirit lifts to a higher plane, not knowing what that plane is or where and not having him in this one wounded me, a wound I knew would take a long time to heal, if ever. I vowed that Litonya and I would do whatever we could to see Elsu into manhood and share memories and Hanta's story with our grandchildren.

Litonya must have sensed my sadness, calling to me, "Come Enyeto, let us eat that you may be hearty for a long tomorrow." She held my hand tightly as we strolled toward the hut pausing here and there to take in the stars illuminating the dark sky directly above us. It seemed they were lighting a path just for us to our hut. I felt a strong sense of my father and grandfather, wondering what adventures awaited our son the next day. As Litonya welcomed sleep, her final words were, "My Elsu had better feel more like a human and less like them when he returns."

We were up early the following day, as was Jenny scouting down the river a little way to check the current. Her keen nose twitched as she sniffed the air for smells or scents that might spell danger.

She was also up for a very different reason, a personal one. She wished to speak to Captain Will. "I'm trying my best to be strong, but I'm unsure right now," she confided. "I could use your help," she said, gazing at a rising sun connecting them both at that moment. "I don't know what's around the corner, but it's my responsibility to lead our crew forward. They all think I'm smart, but I realize leading takes more than that. You were always confident and sure of yourself. Even in the face of danger, you put the crew first. There was no pretending in you, and the crew loved and respected you for that. I want to lead the same way, not as a cute little bunny with all the answers. The crew deserves a fearless leader, and I intend to be that leader for them. Thanks for listening, my friend."

Her words were so compelling they traveled across time and space straight to Will's ears. And she felt he was with her to face whatever came her way. So, when the crew woke from their slumber, they greeted a new Jenny upon her return to the Sitka. They could see in her eyes she had changed. "She looks different," remarked Akoni Raccoon.

"She is different," added Sasha Beaver. "She's Captain Jenny." Her added confidence and swagger made the morning air seem a little crisper.

Jenny entered the cabin where Gio was nudging Jr. and Elsu into the morning. "I'm hungry," whined Jr.

"Me too," grumbled Elsu.

"I wish I could feed my boy," moaned Litonya.

"Okay, kids, go out to the deck," ordered Gio. "The crew is fixing breakfast right now," Off they dashed, bumping into each other to get there first.

Kids will be kids, I chuckled.

As Jenny turned to join them, Gio grabbed her softly by the paw. "I need to say something to you. I think you're doing a great job filling in for Captain Will. And for the record, you're not just some cute little bunny trying to lead a grouchy bunch of critters. I'm sure I speak for the entire crew when I say we love and respect you. So, I just wanted you to know that." Then he softly nuzzled his nose to hers before heading to the deck.

Speechless, Jenny paused to collect herself. Emotions raced through her as a tear trickled down her cheek. Captain

Will had spoken to her through Gio. Now she realized that their destiny was in her capable paws.

With the sun rising fast in the east and every one sporting full tummies, they shoved off downriver. Sasha guided their way through the water while Elsu and Jr. wielded stick swords at the bow pretending to be pirates.

While cruising along, Jenny informed the crew, "We'll probably need to replenish our food supplies during the trip home. The ballast area keeps supplies cool, but not forever. Different types of food must be stored according to the temperatures of different storage areas. At the next stopover, we'll recheck the freshness of everything."

Luckily for Gio, his supply of carrots had a shelf-life way longer than most other produce though he didn't know it. That one brown foot of his must be what is known as a lucky rabbit's foot because all Gio's good fortunes could easily have been misfortunes.

They traveled through the early afternoon, then docked temporarily to check their food supply. The nuts, seeds, and dried and smoked products from Captain John seemed fine, but the fruits and vegetables were starting to wilt. Unexpectantly, Elsu raised his arm, signaling his desire to say something. "Yes, Elsu," acknowledged Jenny.

"Well, this used to happen to my family too. Mom would select the ripest food and make dinner. Then churn some into a thick dressing or tasty paste with nuts and seeds making it last longer. Finally, she would peel off the ripe or wilted layer and use that first so that the leftover parts would last longer."

"Great plan, Elsu. We'll do that once we dock for the night. Your mom is really smart. I'm sure you miss her a lot."

Elsu replied, "Yes, I do, but for now, I still have a really smart mom," causing Jenny to blush a little. Litonya blushed a little too.

"The sun will set in a bit, Captain, so maybe we should dock soon?" suggested Akoni.

"Let's look for a good spot," Jenny responded.

Another fifteen minutes or so upriver, they found a site that seemed ideal and strangely familiar. "Hey," said Amos, "isn't this where we stopped to visit the lagoon? It can't be far away. Let's go surprise Morgan if we can find him."

"Yeah," said Sasha, "that'll give him something to doubletalk about, aark, aark." Everyone laughed at Sasha's little macaw joke.

They maneuvered through the woods until they came to a small clearing bordering the shore of the Lagoon Lake and spectacular waterfall seemingly flowing from the heavens. With the heavy overspray and cooler temperature, it felt like heaven too. "Maybe we should just live here," joked Sasha as he dove into the water to hunt.

They settled down on the shore with their heads tilted skyward, pivoting, looking for Morgan among the tall pines. Although they didn't see him, they certainly heard him and his family with those all too familiar aarks echoing through the lagoon. Amos yelled a double aark as loud as he could, and sure enough, Morgan flew down from a tall tree.

"Boy, you guys are a sight for sore eyes. I was just about to look for the Sitka. What a wonderful surprise, wonderful surprise, yes, it is."

"There's Mr. Doubletalk," shrugged Sasha while munching on some crustacean.

"C'mon, c'mon, you have to meet my family, aark, meet them yes."

John was talking with Harper, his head foreman, at the compound about the gold. "You know, Harper, I didn't feel anything like my special stone in those bags, so they didn't have it. They don't even know what it is, just a bunch of dumb critters who wouldn't have a clue about a magic stone. So, that means we still have to track down the coyotes. Have the men ready in the morning. I've gotta special treat for that ringleader they call Calvin, a very special treat," he repeated, cocking his pistol, then releasing the hammer.

At the lagoon, you could hear Morgan shouting, "C'mon down, c'mon, it's safe," trying to coax his family perched high in a pine tree straddling the lagoon shoreline to fly down. "I want you to meet my other family." But the McCaw family hesitated, surveying the odd collection of would-be predators on the ground.

Finally, they reasoned that the hawk could have easily attacked them already. Plus, Morgan was already on the ground joshing with the crew. So, they left their perch and flew down for introductions.

Afterward, both groups proceeded to a plateau about a third of the way up the waterfall. From there they had a view of the area, and at least a part of the Sitka. Once everyone got comfortable, the wild stories flowed like the cascading water.

Papa Macaw was anxious to spill the beans on Morgan as a little fella. "He was something else," teased Papa. "Always into mischief and the nosiest bird ever. But he did learn to fly quicker than the other hatchlings. I believe he was anxious to eavesdrop on everyone, so he had to fly to get close. Yes, he was a little stinker."

"I knew there was something I liked about Morgan," joked Amos.

Papa McCaw continued, "One day, Mama and I decided to play a little trick on him. We knew he was hiding in a tree near where we were cooling in the overspray of the waterfall. So, I yelled to Mama, did you eat that last carrot in the nest? I was planning on having that later for lunch. Mama yelled back, no, it's still there. Now, carrots are a real treat for any bird but nearly impossible to find."

"We could see the brush move as Morgan bolted straight for our nest home while we laughed our heads off. By the time we returned, Morgan had eaten almost half of what he had thought was a carrot but actually was an orange-tinted wet stick I found at the lagoon that looked like a carrot. I was letting it dry out to use later. Some little bird had quite the tummy ache that night, aark, aark, quite the tummy ache." The MaCaws and Sitka crew broke out in laughter, with brother Lago pointing at Morgan.

"Hey, I've got a story about Mr. can't fly straight," claimed Amos. He described how Morgan flew from one tree limb only to slam into another while executing some eavesdropping undercover work. Again, there was rowdy laughter from the group.

"Hardy har," snickered Morgan. "Well, I've got my own eavesdropping story to top all of yours," he countered. "Quite a while back, before I met you all (raising his left wing at the crew), I was feeling extra bored one day. So, I decided to go eavesdrop on John and his men. I waited till dusk cause they're mouthier and louder after downing a few pints. Easier to hear."

"Captain John mentioned the magic wheat, aark, magic wheat." I heard him tell Harper, "If that darn Mike doesn't find it soon, I'll have to assemble a mining crew to find it, aark find it. Soon a lot of freeloaders will show up. I'll need that stone to be in control of things if you know what I mean," looking straight at Harper. "We're running out of time aark, out of time. Maybe I should have the Indians look for it, eh? They probably know how it works too. What do you think?"

"Harper leaned over with his hand cupped and whispered in John's ear," "We should give old Mike a while longer. I've got a feeling he's getting close. Then we only have to get rid of one that way."

"Yeah, you're right," replied John in a hushed tone. "Ok, we'll keep things status quo for now."

"And the funny thing is they had no idea I was right there listening to every word, aark, every word through an open window. I was sitting right on the window ledge. I mean, how did they not see me? Isn't that the funniest thing? I was right there, ark, right there."

Morgan didn't even notice that Captain Jenny and the whole crew were standing now, ears fully erect, understanding the gravity of his story. Looking at each other, they said almost in unison, "It's getting late. We'd better get back to the Sitka."

"See ya tomorrow bright and early, Morgan?" asked Jenny.

"I'll be raring to go, yes, to go." The crew hastily left Morgan and his family for the Sitka to have a serious discussion.

"What did you think of Morgan's story?" Jenny asked the crew, noticeably concerned.

"I don't think it was another one of his whoppers," said Jonathan. "If John gets the Miwoks to find it, he might discover how the whole thing works with the cave and everything. With Notaku gone, they may be in grave danger."

"But it didn't seem like he had the stone before we left with his snooping through all the bags of gold. So, I'm sure he hasn't got it," replied Jenny. "And he's sure we haven't got it, or he wouldn't have let us leave."

"You think we should've taken the stone with us?" Johnathan asked, continuing, "But if we did that, how would Will, Owen, Notaku, and Warrick get back?"

"I don't think it works that way," asserted Jenny. "Otherwise, they would've had to take the stone with them, which is impossible since there's just one stone as far as we know. Right?" she declared, looking at the crew.

"Right," they agreed.

Jenny continued, "My vote is we continue our journey home. We'll figure out what to do once we get there." Her plan was a popular proposal with the crew longing for home. They all gave Jenny the thumbs up. She knew in her gut that returning home was not only the smart but correct decision. But she also knew they'd have to return to New Helvetia sooner than later.

"Speaking of home, Captain, how long do you think it'll take us to get there?" asked Joaquin.

That question caught everyone's interest as they leaned in to hear the answer. "The currents and tide are always shifting," she replied. "I believe they funnel mostly out to sea. So, our trip home should be faster than when we came, barring unforeseen delays. Tomorrow's a busy day, so let's get some shuteye."

As Jenny turned toward the cabin, her eyes doing a quick last scan of the woods, she thought she saw some kind of glitching, spindly shadow near some trees. Or was it just the light of the moon flickering through the trees? *I must truly be tired*, she thought. *Now I'm seeing things that aren't even there*. Or was it?

Chapter 10
A Mysterious Stranger

The next morning of day three would be another exciting venture dubbed, Scrub the Deck quest. Yes, it was cleaning day. After all, this is a crew of hairy, furry animals. Morgan and Joaquin, as flyers, were not physically equipped for this quest, so they pulled watch duty. The rest would clean and rotate turns manning the helm. Elsu moaned, "This is familiar," reflecting on his mother badgering him to clean his area and help with chores. But, at least they would dock early this day to forage for food.

The Sitka cruised along comfortably, engine humming, steam bellowing from its smokestack. Sasha hollered up to Jenny manning her turn at the rudder, "Shipwreck ahead; shipwreck ahead, starboard side." Momentarily, she considered stopping to rummage the same wreck they did coming. But she dismissed the thought, seeing even more booby and other birds than last time.

That didn't stop Joaquin from crash-diving the birds a few times. Though many birds take flight with a predator diving at them, the booby birds didn't budge or flinch. *They're lucky I just finished lunch*, he mused.

Once the Sitka docked, Jenny, Morgan, and Sasha stayed aboard to guard it while minding the kids. The rest of the crew headed out to search for food.

A short distance into the woods, Amos shouted at Akoni, "Did you see that?"

"See what?" replied Akoni with a puzzled look.

"It was right there, darted past the trees." Akoni scampered over to the area Amos was pointing at to look around. Leaning down, he picked up a long feather. "Nothing here except this," holding it up for Amos to see.

"Maybe it was just a big bird," joked Akoni, prompting a scowl from Amos.

"You're being funny when I tell you I saw something," repeated Amos.

"Well, see if you can see some food. We can't return empty-handed. C'mon."

The foragers did manage to find quite a few tasty goodies. Some walnuts, juicy plums, wild blueberries and some weird-looking fruit they later figured out was kiwi. With some of Captain John's smoked meats, dinner turned out to be quite pleasing that evening. But I can tell you this. That would not be the last of the big bird joking.

"Oh, Captain Jenny, Sasha wants to tell you about the big bird he spotted running through the forest," shared Akoni. "He tried to catch him, but the bird was too fast for his stubby legs."

"That's not funny," retorted Sasha, spinning around quickly to confront Akoni.

"Now boys, settle down," Jenny counseled. Then, she turned to Sasha, trying to shield Akoni with her body, asking in a hushed tone, "So you saw something?"

"Sure thing, Captain. I think it was human, but it moved so fast I didn't get a good look at it."

"Ok, thanks, Sasha. We can't be too careful."

"I agree, Captain," replied Sasha, casting a defiant gaze Akoni's way.

That might have been a joke to Akoni but not to Jenny. She connected it to the shadowy figure she spotted the night before but had dismissed it as her tiredness. *Something's following us,* she thought. *Can't be another Warrick if it looked human, but Sasha's not sure.* Jenny kept running things over and over in her mind.

Won't alarm the crew, but need to keep a sharp lookout. I'll have Joaquin help. Understanding the gravity of this potential new threat, Joaquin perched himself high in a pine tree early that evening to begin his vigil.

As night fell and the rest of the crew retired for sleep, Jenny faked needing to adjust the tiller. But, she was really scanning the area for the mysterious creature or person, a threat either way in her mind. Simultaneously, the mysterious entity was eyeing the Sitka from the woods, looking for…what? No one knows.

The only certainty was neither Joaquin, Jenny, nor the mysterious creature noticed master eavesdropper Morgan perched high on a tree branch directly behind everyone watching. *So, it's not a bird,* Morgan said to himself. *It's a feathery human.* Overhearing Morgan's comment to himself, the entity bolted into the night. Morgan's eavesdropping talent was already starting to pay dividends.

Morgan zoomed back to the Sitka so fast he hit the tea kettle, knocking its top onto the deck. It landed, nearly hitting Gio doing lifeguard duties as the kids took one last swim near the boat before dinner. "Hey, you need to slow down," complained Gio. "That's the second time you've hit that tea kettle."

"Where's Captain Jenny? Where's Captain Jenny?" asked Morgan in a panic. "I've got important news for her, important news."

"She's back by the rudder. Go easy before you hurt somebody."

But Morgan was already doing a fast-paced parrot shuffle toward the rudder. "It's human, a feathery human, I say, in the forest."

"You're sure?" Jenny questioned. Getting an affirmative response from Morgan, she rewarded him with a promotion from eavesdropper to detective.

"Detective Morgan, Detective Morgan," he repeated. "I like the ring of that." He strode to the bow to brag about his new title to the crew.

Jenny called Joaquin from the tree to inform him of Morgan's discovery. *Now I'll have to tell the whole crew before Morgan does*, she reasoned. *At least, everyone can be on high alert now.*

It was getting late, so Gio called Elsu and Jr. in from swimming to eat and get ready for sleep time. This night, it would be Elsu's turn to share a story. Luckily, he had many shared with him by Grandpa and me. After drying off, the kids cuddled in some blankets in the cabin. Then, Elsu began his favorite story for the rabbit family told him by Grandpa Liwanu, who told it to me when I was about Elsu's age.

Once, two little boys living in the valley went down to the river to swim. After paddling and splashing about to their heart's content, they went on shore and crept up on a huge boulder that stood beside the water. They lay down in the warm sunshine to dry themselves but fell asleep. They slept so soundly that they knew nothing, though the great boulder grew day by day and rose night by night until it lifted them up beyond the sight of their tribe, who looked for them everywhere.

The rock grew until the boys were lifted high into the heaven. Even far up above the blue sky until they scraped their faces against the moon. And still, year after year, among the clouds, they slept.

Then, all the animals held a great council to bring the boys down from the top of the great rock. Every animal leaped as high as he could up the face of the rocky wall. Mouse could only jump as high as one's hand. Rat, twice as big tried. Then Raccoon tried: he could jump a little farther. One after another, the animals tried, and Grizzly Bear made a great leap far up the wall but fell back.

Last, of all, Lion tried and jumped farther than any other animal but fell down upon his back. Then came tiny Measuring-Worm, and began to creep up the rock. Soon he reached as high as Raccoon had jumped, then as high as Bear, then as high as Lion's leap, and by and by, he was out of sight, climbing up the face of the rock. So, Measuring-Worm climbed the rock for one whole snow and finally reached the top. Then he awakened the boys and came down the same way he went up and brought them safely to the ground. My grandpa said that is why the rock is called Tutokanula, the measuring worn.

Elsu barely finished his tale before dozing off. "That was a beautiful story," whispered Jenny, gazing lovingly at the two kids; Elsu probably counting sheep, Jr. probably counting carrots. Gio and Jenny briefly chatted about the mystery human before drifting off to sleep.

The next day was unusually ordinary for a change with Sasha's mint tea with breakfast, Elsu and Jr. swimming, and the adults lounging on the deck lifeguarding. Then, some scouting before lunch, stargazing at night, and no sign of the mysterious entity.

The day after was a completely different story. The top priority was foraging enough food to make it to Yerba Buena Island by the next day without depleting their stored supplies. The idea of home was abuzz. But the events of this day would make that the last thing on the crew's mind.

The morning began as usual. A little warmer than in past days, so birds were out early, chirping and darting for morsels to eat or just singing in a new day. Small critters were dashing about on the ground, keeping Joaquin occupied, trying to catch breakfast.

Elsu and Jr. overslept, so they wound up having an early lunch before hitting the river. The Sitka had docked in a small cove, so it was like having a private lake to swim in. Once they dried off, though, Gio Jr. wanted to go up the shore further to explore, convincing Elsu to tag along. Gio, doing supervision duties from the deck, yelled, "Don't go too far," figuring with Elsu along, Jr. would stay out of trouble.

They shuffled along the bank where it jutted back out to the river, then in again to form another larger swimming cove still in partial view of the Sitka. So, they figured they were safe. But, as they neared the water, to their surprise, knee-deep on the other side of the cove trying to spear a fish was a human wearing a feathery headband. He smiled and waved at them. Gio Jr. was already in scamper mode, remembering what happened before with Warrick Wolf. But Elsu grabbed his paw, saying, "Wait a second, Jr. It's alright. He's just an Indian hunting for supper."

"You sure?" replied a nervous Gio Jr., hiding behind Elsu. "Okay."

They stayed in shallow water, a safe distance from the stranger and watched him throw a few somethings in, then wait on shore. A few minutes later, some fish floated to the top that he grabbed and disappeared into the forest, waving to them as he left.

It was a strange, unsettling sensation for Gio Jr. Still, Elsu felt surprisingly comfortable, almost drawn to the stranger. Maybe, because he was the first human he'd seen in days. Or, perhaps it was because the stranger looked Indian like him. Or maybe it was something else?

"Enyeto, can't you see that the stranger would draw our son to him? I am sure he is missing us, the village, his friends, and his life here at home. If I could only tell him I love him, miss holding him and tucking him to bed at night," Litonya sobbed.

I knew I had to take a break to hold my wife close and comfort her. "He will return to us soon, Litonya. But, for now, we must embrace his adventures, for he shall return to us changed. His experiences will grow him. He will not return as the Elsu who left, and we must accept that." And he will sense that we will not be the parents he left. All will be different while remaining the same. He shall always be our Elsu, and we, his parents. This bond that shall endure till time ceases. Litonya composed herself, so I continued the story, curious about the stranger with feathers.

By now, Gio was calling to them, "Hey, you two, get back over by the boat where I can see you better." They complied but played a little longer before climbing on deck.

Later, during dinner, Gio Jr. blurted out, "Hey Mom, guess what we saw today? C'mon, guess?"

"A whale?" guessed Jenny.

"NO," replied Jr.

"A giant carrot then?"

"No, Mom, not a carrot."

"A pony?" tried Jenny.

"Mommm, what would a pony be doing in the river? Guess right this time."

"Ok, I give up. What did you guys see today?"

"A man with feathers," replied Jr., enjoying the look of shock on his mom's face.

Jenny nearly choked on her food, staring straight at Gio as the rest of the crew chuckled, shifting to faraway spots on the deck. "Is this true, Elsu?" she asked, who confirmed the whole encounter, attaching a description to it.

Jenny, up on all fours, now quickly moved toward Joaquin. "Take Akoni, Jonathan, and Amos and scour the area right now. Don't confront the stranger if you see him. Just observe and report back pronto. We don't know what we're dealing with."

Then Elsu chimed in, "He didn't look dangerous to me, just fishing. He reminded me of the scouts from my village. I don't think he'd harm us."

"We'll see," said Jenny. "We'll see."

The scouts returned empty-handed, so she pulled Joaquin aside from the earshot of the other crew members. "I want you to do a flyover later for anything resembling a campfire."

"You got it, Captain," replied Joaquin.

He's got to cook that fish sometime, she reasoned. But she didn't have time to worry about that right now. It was foraging time.

"Everyone on deck right away," ordered Captain Jenny. Once the crew arrived, the forage planning session commenced. By sheer coincidence, they were near the same pastures where Gio had executed his self-proclaimed great escape from the guard dogs.

Chapter 11
Here We Go Again

"You know, we did pretty well coming, so long as Gio stays away from that carrot patch," Jonathan joked.

"That's true," answered Jenny smiling. "But now we have Elsu. He can carry more with his hands and arms than any of us. Plus, he can see over the top of the crop fields."

"Good thinking," said Akoni. "If I may suggest, let's have Amos spy on those guard dogs. They wouldn't dare mess with him (Amos smiling wryly). Then, we can position Morgan in a tree nearby with a wide view of the crop fields so he can do one of his warning aarks. Everyone will hear that. It might distract the dogs for a minute or two. So, who are you thinking about as the foraging team?"

Jenny thought. "Well, we'll need speed and quickness. Any volunteers?"

Most of the crew stepped backward, leaving Akoni, Jonathan, and Gio unwittingly on the hook. "There's our team," she decided. "But I'll have to be on-site to coordinate, so Gio, will you stay with Jr. this time? Please?"

"No worries," replied Gio.

"Thanks," replied Jenny blowing a kiss in his direction that he caught and patted on his cheek.

Turning back to the rest of the crew, Jenny explained, "At dusk, we'll make our way close to the crop fields and execute the same plan as before with some new wrinkles. My husband will NOT be used as bait to lure vicious guard dogs away this time (she had never been excited about that plan). Instead, Gio will stand duty guarding the Sitka. We'll take some of John's dried meats to keep the dogs busy while Amos stands guard nearby. Then position Morgan as we discussed earlier. I'll keep watch while you three (pointing at Jonathan, Akoni, and Elsu) make two fast trips and fill the gunny sacks. If we carefully pull this off, no one should get in harm's way. That's the plan. Any questions?"

Litonya interrupted, asking, "Why does Jenny have Elsu go to the pastures? He's just a boy. Why put him in harm's way? I know what you're going to tell me, Enyeto. He's growing into a man through his experiences. But I cannot bear to witness this episode where he can be hurt. I just cannot. Retrieve me when Jenny's plan is concluded. I will be in our hut."

As she left, I thought to myself, a mother will always be a mother, and a son, even as a man, will always be her little boy.

Back to the plan, everyone nodded in agreement, but Amos raised his paw with a question. "What about Joaquin? What's he doing all this time?"

"Oh yeah, I almost forgot. He'll be doing air surveillance. Right, Joaquin?" glancing his way. Joaquin nodded to Jenny in the affirmative. So, the plan was set. Now the wait. The long agonizing wait. Most forest animals are quick to think and even quicker to act. Everyone was excited but on edge, so a little snappy. Failure was not an option. Though, in the back of Jenny's mind dwelled the X factor, the stranger. What are his motives?

Dusk seemed like it would never come but arrive it did. Jenny double-checked with everyone to ensure they understood their roles, especially Joaquin's dual one. I was on edge with anticipation, and so were the villagers listening. I could see Litonya nervously glancing from the hut for a signal that the plan had worked and Elsu was safe. But, unfortunately, that signal would have to wait.

The crew set out for the crop fields with just a smidgeon of day left. "Just don't seem right, us hiding here while Mom takes all the risks," complained Gio Jr., looking squarely at his dad.

For the first time, Gio realized his son was no longer a kid, as rabbits grow up fast. Quickly, he thought up a plan. Jr. could tell so wisely; he gave dad a little space. "I've got it," spouted Gio. "We'll sneak down near the crop fields and provide backup if they need it. Then, if they have everything under control, we can hightail it back to the cabin like we never left." Jr. liked this idea, clapping his paws together in approval, so off they went.

Being rabbits, they caught up to them quickly and then intentionally lagged behind, not that the crew would notice, concentrating solely on the mission ahead. Jr. whispered, "This is fun, like hunting the hunters."

"Shh, concentrate," Gio whispered. "This is serious. We've got to be ready."

"Roger that," answered Jr. in a low voice.

"Roger that?" Gio repeated, staring at his son. *Where did he learn that? Maybe he is still a kid*, but Gio had to admit that he was also excited by this little rogue mission.

So, the plot was set with all the players except one. Where was the stranger?

Moonlight cascaded over the farmhouse and fields. Unexpectedly, the farm owner, his family, and their two guard dogs were relaxing on the front porch taking in the pleasant evening. Jenny motioned with her left paw held high, the FREEZE sign, meaning, don't move from your posts. For the moment, the itchy, triggered crew had to exhale and wait. "I knew this plan wouldn't work," complained Amos. "We should just go."

"Keep quiet, Amos. Have a little faith," said Akoni. A few minutes later, a welcome sight. The family and two guard dogs went inside. They left the front door open, so air could pass through their crude, homemade screen door.

"This is perfect," murmured Jenny, "both dogs inside." Then, with her right paw raised high, she signaled the GO sign to the crew, and their plan was in synchronized motion. Amos adjusted the angle of his position slightly to view the front door. Joaquin looped overhead, looking for the campfire and watching for action on the ground. Morgan, perched in an observation position, remained silent for the time being as Akoni, Jonathan, and Elsu were bee-lining to the fields. But there would be a couple of flies in the ointment.

Akoni, Jonathan, and Elsu completed round one to and from the crop fields lugging gunny sacks filled to the brim. However, trip two involved some unexpected drama. First, Joaquin started wildly flapping his wings at Jenny, signaling something. But what? And those dogs inside the house, their senses were aroused by unfamiliar scents wafting through the screen door. Agitated, they began howling and barking to go outside. Finally, Joaquin flew down to Jenny to advise her, "I saw the campfire about 100 yards that way, pointing toward the woods. But I didn't see anybody near it."

Hearing the anxious howling of the dogs, Morgan let out an ear-piercing aark alerting everyone of a problem. Some children hopped into their parent's laps as Amos backed his way onto the edge of the porch. He released a tiny bit of his magic, trying to trick the mutts and their owners into thinking it was just a skunk outside, nothing to be alarmed about. That worked for a few minutes until the owners peering out a window, saw the Sitka thieves stealing their goods. "Go get 'em," they yelled, opening the screen door.

One dog bolted straight at Jonathan as he was more uprightly visible. Akoni found a new speed gear darting back to the woods, even hauling a partially filled sack. The other dog was tracking toward our son, who didn't even notice the beast till he was about 10 feet away. Some of the kids listening yelled for Elsu to run.

My heart was in my throat and I could feel myself panting. However, I knew I had to continue, so I sucked in some air and went on. Elsu immediately dropped his sack and began slowly moving backward, keeping an eye on the growling monster creeping toward him. I too yelled, "Run, Elsu, run," as if he could hear me. But he tripped over one of the dirt rows and fell on his back.

I cringed and couldn't help but turn away as the dog, with his fangs bared, took this opportunity to lunge at my boy. Elsu closed his eyes, turned his head, and raised his left forearm in a defensive position. Father and I had taught him this tactic to avoid suffering a mortal wound to a vital body part, give up the arm.

He waited for contact that never came. He heard a grunt, then a loud thud while his eyes were shut tight. My eyes were closed too out of fear for our son. Slowly, he sat up, peering to check his predicament. He was shocked to see the feather-headed stranger crouching over the dog stretched out between two rows of lettuce, out cold.

"You okay?" The stranger asked, extending an arm to help Elsu to his feet.

"You okay?" the village parents asked, sensing my distress by what was happening to Elsu.

I waved to them, signaling all was fine, then took a deep breath before continuing. "Better vamoose before the farmer comes out with his gun," warned the stranger, moving toward the part of the woods where Joaquin had spotted the campfire.

Elsu grabbed his spilled sack, heart beating a mile a minute, and raced back to where the crew was hiding. Luckily for Jonathan, Joaquin deterred his attacker, swooping down with razor-sharp claws to the hiney.

Jenny, who witnessed all the action, shouted, "Everyone back to the Sitka pronto." The whimpering dogs limped their way back to the farmhouse, posing as victors hoping to get tasty treats as their reward for subduing the intruders.

At this point, I took a minute to settle my emotions and wave Litonya back from the hut. I'd never seen her move that swiftly. Her feet barely touched the ground like she was riding a current of air to the story tree. I updated her on what she had missed. It was a good thing she was sitting down on the soft pine needles.

Back at the Sitka, the crew felt gratified this venture didn't go entirely sideways. Elsu restated, "See! I told you the stranger was okay. He saved me, so we owe him, right?"

"Yes, Elsu, I am thankful he showed up when he did. I couldn't bear the thought of anything happening to either of you," glancing at Jr., then back at Elsu. "I owe him and your mother too. Till you return to her, I vow to keep you safe and out of harm's way." I could see this gave Litonya some peace of mind.

As Jenny hugged them tightly for a long minute, she thought of Warrick Wolf. Then, she had the crew store the bounty in the ballast area with the other supplies. Gio cruised out of the cabin yawning, "How'd it go?"

"Just two vicious guard dogs chasing us through the crop fields," replied Akoni. "Nothing you couldn't handle."

Master detective eavesdropper filled them in on all the particulars, to which Gio commented, "Where's a speedy rabbit when you need him," smirking at his wife, who found that amusing.

"Let's just thank our ancestral spirits harm came to no one," offered Jenny. They observed a silent moment of thanks. Then, suddenly, it dawned on them, "We could be home by tomorrow. Tomorrow!"

"That wasn't me, wasn't me," mused Morgan, drawing a chuckle from all.

There would be no stargazing or tall tales about whose star was the best, brightest, or anything tonight. Instead, everyone reflected on their family on Yerba Buena Island.

"Should not our son be thinking about family and desire to return to us?"

To which I answered, "Litonya, he will return when he is ready to return. That does not mean he loves us or misses us less. He is your son, Litonya, and your son only. Nothing or no one can break this bond." I knew I was stating what she already knew but needed to hear. She gazed at me lovingly for that as the story went on.

Jenny couldn't help getting caught up in the hoopla about home. Also, she couldn't help wondering about Elsu's hero stranger and his whereabouts, wishing she could thank him in person for his bravery. But at this point, he seemed more like a ghost than an actual person.

Chapter 12
Unexpected Encounter

Then, as if someone was answering her prayers, there he stood on the bank, his left palm pressed against a tree trunk with a pointed sphere grasped tightly in his right. She flinched for a moment, then quickly recovered to summon a smile and a wave to him that he cautiously acknowledged.

She motioned him to come aboard, but he seemed understandably reluctant. I mean, an odd collection of animals on a floating contraption he'd never seen before spewing smoke. So, she had the entire crew with Elsu in front wave him aboard and that worked.

Hesitantly, he stepped onto the deck by the bow to allow him a quick retreat if needed. "I was just wondering if the boy was okay?" he asked in an almost reverent tone.

With a big smile, Elsu stretched out his hand to fully welcome his hero. I found my hand unconsciously stretching out to the stranger causing the villagers to sigh joyfully. I would have embraced him if I could, as would Litonya, for saving our son's life. He was our hero as well.

Most of the crew had reseated to resume reminiscing about family and friends. Elsu and the stranger joined them seated with their legs folded beneath them. "Wow! Look at that," Akoni exclaimed. "They sit the same way. Must be an Indian thing."

"I am called Moleemo," the stranger told them. "My grandfather named me."

"You are Miwok like me?" asked Elsu excitedly, peering up at the stranger.

"Yes, little one," Moleemo confirmed. "You and I are tribal family, brethren in spirit. I was hopeful you survived the attack dogs. However, my worry compelled me to come forth. Thankfully, our ancestor's hand guided your well-being."

"Well, so did your hand. Thank you," added Elsu, gesturing with his right hand over his heart as Moleemo did the same. Elsu felt a warmth inside, recalling how he and Grandpa Liwanu would exchange the same special gesture with each other sometimes.

This part of the story stirred something deep inside me that I could not explain. It took me a little time to resume talking. Finally, I did.

"Please, Moleemo, have something to eat," offered Jenny, paw outstretched with a bowl of fruit. "Join us. Please?" which he did.

"So, where are you from?" inquired Jonathan. "Up North near Captain John's territory?"

"I know not of a Captain John," replied Moleemo. "These parts look familiar to me, then not. I am unsure why, but my memory is conflicted as if I existed in shared time and space, but now, I am here in this time. I've been attempting to make sense of this mystery. Right now, I have not the answers."

Gio whispered to Jenny, "He sounds just like Captain Will. Maybe we should take him with us?"

Jenny agreed, so she issued an invitation that Moleemo accepted. Elsu was thrilled to have another human on board, and a Miwok to boot, even if he was older than him.

In typical Miwok tradition, Moleemo was an honorable, noble soul, ready to contribute his fair share to the Sitka's well-being. And, like Sasha, he was a masterful fisherman, adding more fresh catches to their meals.

With cramped deck space, fortunately, they didn't have far to reach Yerba Buena. So, Elsu and Moleemo offered to sleep on the cabin's roof. That way, they could share stories. And what stories they had.

Elsu couldn't wait to tell Moleemo the story Grampa Liwanu was telling him, his father, and his mother. That is, before he morphed into it, a story on its own. Moleemo was spellbound as Elsu described how a young Liwanu and some friends took their tule boats to Yerba Buena Island, where they were heading. Elsu continued, explaining how Liwanu heard Will the bear talking with some animals about a journey somewhere. Then, with Moleemo hanging on every word, Elsu recounted the whole story about Hanta, his great-grandfather, as told to him by Grandpa Liwanu.

"Hanta told Liwanu that when he was a young hunter, he found a helpless cub bear one day. Trappers had killed its mother. So, he wrapped him in a blanket, took him home, and raised him. Can you believe that?" said Elsu. "Raising a bear?" Elsu continued with the story. "Over time, he learned to love the bear, and the bear grew to love him back."

Moleemo said, "That's not as unusual as you think. Our people have great respect and reverence for the earth and its creatures. But talking animals, I have never experienced or even heard of that before. Please go on, Elsu."

"Well, according to Grandpa Liwanu, they became so close it was like they could read each other's minds. But the cub grew up fast, so Hanta had to let it go. That's when the bear spoke and said, 'Hanta, thank you for rescuing me. I owe you my life. You and I will always have a connection. From this day on, you will always know what I know, see what I see, and feel what I feel'."

"What a blessing," commented Moleemo, still trying to digest this remarkable story.

"And that's not the half of it," added Elsu, pausing to build suspense. "Guess who Will the bear is? Guess!" Then, not waiting for a reply, he exclaimed, "Captain Will, captain of the Sitka, the boat we're on right now."

Moleemo responded, "That's an amazing story, Elsu," while somewhere in his mind, it had scratched a memory. Then, snapping back into the present, he asked, "Where is Captain Will now? It looks like the Sitka has a captain."

"Yes, Captain Jenny. But she's just filling in till he returns," explained Elsu.

Of course, this triggered the saga of Captain Will, Owen, Notaku, and Warrick Wolf and how they had transported somewhere. "This story just keeps getting better," said Moleemo. At that, Elsu rattled on about the battle in the crop fields, Calvin and the coyotes, the quest for gold, and even the mysterious nugget and its magical properties.

The more Elsu talked, the clearer Moleemo's memories became. Frame by frame, his whole life was coming into focus, overwhelming him. So much to take in that he could barely breathe. It was at that moment that all became clear. Then, he gazed upon his grandson with love and emotions spilling over like the waterfalls at Morgan's lagoon. Tears of joy and revelation welled in his eyes, realizing his existence in the other time dimension had ended, and this was his existence now, his life. But then there was Elsu to consider, losing a grandfather to gain a grandfather, a confusing dilemma for a ten-year-old.

"What's wrong, Moleemo?" asked Elsu.

Moleemo looked into Elsu's eyes, answering, "That's not my real name, Son, or shall I call you grandson?"

"What are you talking about? My grandpa's name is Liwanu. He passed on. But he was kinda my best friend."

"Elsu, look into my eyes. My name is Liwanu. It's me, Grandpa."

"That's impossible," claimed Elsu, leaping onto the deck in total denial.

While Elsu tried to process this incredible revelation or untruth, Gio banged on the cabin ceiling, yelling, "Hey, trying to sleep down here." Unfortunately, Elsu and Moleemo, Liwanu, or whomever he was, had lost track of time, so they tabled their talk till morning.

Elsu tried to sleep, but his mind was reeling with questions. Once he settled down, he reasoned that anything was possible if he could transport into the story. But he wasn't quite ready to swallow Moleemo's story that he was Grandpa Liwanu. He would sleep lightly off and on this night, dreaming about his grandpa, then thinking about the one lying next to him, A baffling circumstance for a ten-year-old.

Litonya and I were stunned, speechless. "He is not Moleemo? He is Liwanu, my father?" I cried out with excitement, disbelief, and confusion, trying to process what I had just learned. Even the villagers looked startled. "Please," I said, waving as they shifted away to give us space. Then turning to Litonya, "But we witnessed his end, both of us together. Did we not?"

"We witnessed Liwanu's transformation, Enyeto. Not his death. We must look beyond earthly existence to the spiritual realm, where all things are possible. Are we not seeing our son's story unfold in another plane? Then why not Liwanu too?"

Litonya's explanation that Father and Elsu found each other beyond our domain gave me great joy. "Now, your father will watch over his grandson," Litonya explained. "All is well as well can be. Now, you must continue the story, Enyeto," which I did with renewed optimism.

The following day, everyone was up super early but for different reasons. Elsu was anxious to resume talking with Moleemo, Grandpa, or whoever he was. The crew knew if they finished breakfast and chores early, it would leave more traveling time to get home sooner.

"Joaquin, I want you to fly ahead and signal me the moment the island comes into view," instructed Jenny.

"You got it, Captain."

So today promised to be a spectacular day. Cloudless blue skies beckoned the Sitka home, and the current seemed to be drawing them in too. The Sitka made record speed for a small, tipsy pony boat, as people called her.

On this day, though, center stage was a conversation of conversations as Elsu challenged Moleemo, "Now, explain to me how you're my grandpa." Deep down inside, he desired and felt this to be true. As Moleemo talked, in Elsu's mind, he was slowly transforming into Grandpa Liwanu.

He described me and Litonya, even my broken pinkie finger from a hunting accident that left a lump at my knuckle. Next, he described our hut and everything inside, including Grandpa Liwanu's sleeping quarters. Then, he mentioned the aroma of lavender he loved that slightly wafted into Elsu's side, connecting them while they slept. Then, the clincher. Moleemo related the entire story that Grandpa Liwanu was telling Elsu before passing and awakening in the story. "Only Grandpa would know that hunter boy," reminded Liwanu with a wry smile.

Then in a more serious tone, he explained, "Understand, Elsu. Now that I am here, I cannot return home. You understand, my boy?" It took a few moments for Elsu to grasp, but he reached peace with this situation.

I'm sure he hoped we had too. From then on, they were inseparable. For Elsu, it felt like being with me and Grandfather at the same time. It was a warm feeling for me, like being with Father and Elsu at that moment for me. Then Litonya leaned over and whispered in my ear something I had not even thought of. "Maybe your mom will show up in the story?"

Chapter 13
Home Sweet Home

By late morning, Captain Jenny was considering docking somewhere later in the day when Joaquin swooped down to the tea kettle with a welcome announcement. "I saw home about a half day from here, Captain."

"That's wonderful news, Joaquin. Did you all hear that? We're almost there. Maybe we should dock shy of home and arrive in the morning to be fresh for all the hoopla." The crew agreed, so the Sitka continued upriver till early evening, looking for a convenient place to dock. Finally, they located a sliver of a cove among the oak and willow trees, roses, and tangle of greenery they marveled at on the trip out.

All seemed well with plentiful supplies, a gold hoard, strange trinkets, a Miwok scout and boy, and, most importantly, the crew intact, except for Will and Owen off on a different adventure. They also had Morgan McCaw, master eavesdropper. And what a collection of unbelievable stories they had to tell.

Unexpected was encountering an Indian scouting foursome from the other side of Yerba Buena Island. Who knew they'd be out near where the Sitka docked though

Jenny recalled seeing humans gandering at them from this area when they departed on their journey. *Now what?* she wondered. But Liwanu and Elsu quickly stepped forward to engage them in their native tongue.

"We know of the forest animals residing on the backside of our island," the scouts told them. "We have no desire to harm them. Yerba Buena affords an abundance of consumable gifts and many offerings from the bay waters. We've no need to hunt our neighbors. Occasionally, we harvest a few furs and pelts from those who trespass to steal from us, but even then, only to shelter our elders and young. Animals who can converse with us are revered, and no harm will come at our hands."

This group exuded such sincerity that Jenny decided to invite them to dinner. So Liwanu and Elsu escorted the group onboard a vessel they could never have imagined. They were awed by the smokestack and how the paddle wheels worked. And they didn't quite get the entire logic of the rudder and tiller. And the boiler completely baffled them.

It was a productive evening, though. Great conversation and some bonding between Liwanu, Elsu, and the guests. Surprisingly talk steered toward consideration of a covenant of mutual restraint between inhabitants of both sides of the island. The scouting party agreed to propose to the tribal leaders that all villagers would honor the animal side of Yerba Buena, banning hunting or harvesting. Likewise, the animals would honor the Miwok's side refraining from poaching goods and trespassing. Enforceability would be challenging, but at least it was a start.

Obviously, it would be impossible to corral all the island creatures to adhere to this agreement because animals will be animals. But still, it would be a remarkable victory for the animal population and Jenny and the crew realized that. First, of course, the covenant had to be approved by the Tribal Elders.

The scouting party thanked their animal hosts for a most exhilarating evening and tasty eats. Then, they faded into one of those stunning Yerba Buena sunsets. Although the Sitka crew decided to call it a night, Liwanu and Elsu couldn't resist reliving some past family escapades before retiring. All Jenny could think of was home.

> Going home, can you believe it, were going home.
> Just can't wait to be heading home,
> It's like a dream, but it's for real, soon, we'll be home.
>
> For this I've longed, sweet remedy for us forlorn,
> I'm going home where I belong.
>
> Far and wide, we've journeyed to distant corners,
> Our eyes betrayed by nowhere places,
> Salvaging through difficult paces,
> Sitka, take me to familiar spaces.
>
> Home beseeches me to answer, her message firm,
> Where are those simpler places, joys be known,
> Throng of homespun faces so dear to me,
> Sitka, I yearn for home.

Miles upon miles we've traveled
Venturing, searching afar,
Stalking adventure and fortune,
Yes, we wandered too far,
Risking all, chasing an elusive star

Voices beckon me, time to return
To place familiar, family and friends aching I am
to hold them, soak in their beloved faces,
Seems I've had my fill of exotic places,

Sitka, carry me home.

The following day, everyone was up early to spiffy themselves up for the homecoming extravaganza they expected. But, of course, they were totally deaf to the fact that no one knew they were arriving. "Wait till they see the awesome stuff we brought back," boasted Amos.

"Tonight, I'll build the biggest, most fantastic bonfire ever," added Sasha. "And wait till they see my cool spectacles."

"Well, I can't wait to show off my new son," said Gio, knowing he'd topped them all.

Captain Jenny spoke up, "We must be thankful given what we've seen and been through. So many experiences could have turned disastrous," looking straight at her son. "Remember, we are still without Captain Will and Owen Owl. We've endured natural and unnatural experiences that have changed us forever. We've negotiated for our very lives with humans and discovered gold. Hopefully, we've made a pact with Miwok neighbors to ensure liberty for all

Yerba Buenians. We should be thankful and humble returning to our beloved island home. Let's not just show our family and friends the stuff we brought back. Let's show them the stuff we're made of. We are the crew of the Sitka. This journey may be ending, but our story's just beginning."

The crew was emotionally moved and uplifted by Captain Jenny's words. They looked at each other with renewed devotion and pride, recognizing they weren't just a pack of animals anymore. They were family. "I still can't wait to show everyone all that gold," Akoni whispered to Amos.

"Me too, since I'll have six extra gold pieces," snickered Amos, reminding Akoni of their bet in the woods.

As the Sitka slowly drifted toward the shore, the Miwok scout patrol presented the covenant idea to the Tribal Elders. A couple opposed it, their rationale being their sacred native doctrine to live in harmony with the environment taking what was needed to survive. That included hunting animals for food, clothing, and protection. That was their way. But they were overruled by the majority Tribal Council, who admonished them. The council proclaimed, "We may continue to hunt on our side of the island and the peninsula, fish in the bay and waterways, and harvest anywhere except the animal's home. Certainly, we can live while honoring this covenant for the sake of this small, extraordinary group of talking animals, their family, and friends. Our ancestral spirits command as much from us."

Although the Council had decided, it did not know the sinister intent of the two elders' votes. They'd already confided to each other, "How much do you think a talking animal is worth?" noting that one of them was a kid rabbit who could speak. "If we can kidnap and breed him, our power will be unchecked, and we can seize control of the Council."

But, for now, they'd have to wait till opportunity knocks on their door. Also, they had no inkling they'd have to deal with a clever, doting, protective mother rabbit and ferocious dad. I can tell you that I'm sure Father and Elsu would have something to say about their dark intentions. The villagers nodded affirmatively.

"Eureka, we're here, we're finally home," shouted the entire crew as they hopped off to tie the Sitka and kissed the ground. Sasha splashed joyfully along the familiar shoreline while Joaquin took flight to get a global view of his island paradise.

It took a few minutes before Amos remarked, "Hey, where's everybody? Where's the party, the hugs, the glad you're homes?" Other than some birds flitting about and rustling from small ground critters in the brush, there was no other sign of life.

"Well," reasoned Gio, "it's not like they knew we were coming. Right?"

But Joaquin knew better. Not only had he scouted the day before looking for the island, but he also landed, giving everyone a heads up. *Just wait till we get to Will's tree. Are they in for a surprise!* So, when they landed and Joaquin went airborne, it wasn't to look over the island. Instead, it was to signal they'd docked.

The crew started unloading the Sitka brooding about the missing welcome home party. Jenny instructed them to move everything by Will's tree near their original meeting spot, leaving the produce in the ballast area to stay fresh. Once they finished and sat down to take a breather, "Surprise, surprise," yelled all the family, friends, and a few newcomers to the island, springing out from behind trees and bushes nearby. They showered the crew with hugs, kisses, and high-fives for making it back home. It was a moment of moments. Then, the attention quickly shifted to all the fabulous stuff the crew brought back.

Gio put on his black stovetop hat, knowing that would draw some interest. "What's that thing?" asked longtime buddy rabbit Archie.

"Here, try one on. I've got a bunch," replied Gio, handing him a tan fedora with a fancy band. "Go ahead, try it," persuaded Gio. They looked at each other, rabbits wearing weird hats, and burst out in laughter.

Looking a little more serious, Archie informed Gio he had something to show him. "Well, where is it?" inquired an anxious Gio.

"You mean, who it is," replied Archie as he motioned over among the crowd of greeters. A young rabbit hopped over, squatting next to Archie, who he introduced as his daughter. "I want you to meet Ayla. She was born after you left on your journey."

Gio motioned for Jr. to come over to introduce the two. Being young, restless rabbits, they hit it off right away. Gio Jr. looked at Ayla more like a buddy to hang out with than a girl. He looked at his dad with that can we go play face that his dad acknowledged. So, he and his new friend were off to play a game of hide and seek. "Don't go too far," Gio cautioned them. But I doubt they heard, and I'm sure Gio didn't really care. They were home.

The rest of the crew were busy showing off their treasures. No one knew what to make of the gold but was mesmerized by it, not to mention Will's chest of strange and curious trinkets. They had never seen a harmonica, candles, or spectacles before.

After the initial hoopla, everyone went to their various dwellings around the woods to rest for later. Gio, Jenny, and Jr. discovered a large, comfortable burrow big enough for the three of them. "Finally, we're home," she wept happily.

Father and Elsu got busy constructing their own hut a short way down from Will's tree.

Tonight would be a grand celebration and closer examination of all the stuff they brought back and division of the gold. Then, the rest of the evening would be spent relaxing around Sasha's roaring campfire, sharing stories about the voyage and all that happened.

They had no idea of all that was going to happen!

www.ingramcontent.com/pod-product-compliance
Lightning Source LLC
Chambersburg PA
CBHW060926140726
47996CB00001B/395